Holly Webb

Puppy Love

Illustrated by Sophy Williams

Contents

www.hollywebbanimalstories.com

STRIPES PUBLISHING
An imprint of the Little Tiger Group
1 Coda Studios, 189 Munster Road,
London SW6 6AW

A paperback original
First published in Great Britain in 2017

ISBN: 978-1-84715-815-4

Lucy the Poorly Puppy

For William and Robin

Chapter One

"Bella's looking so fat!" Lauren peered under the kitchen table at Bella, the family's beagle. She was sitting in amongst everyone's feet, panting and looking rather uncomfortable. Her tummy was huge, and the expression on her face was a bit grumpy.

Dad checked under the table too. "Well, she is due to have the pups any day now. I'll take her temperature later on, to check if it's gone down."

Lauren nodded. They had been taking Bella's temperature every day for the last couple of weeks, as their vet, Mark, had told them it was the best way to tell if the puppies were about to come.

Bella padded heavily out from under the table, and wandered over to her cushion. She took hold of the edge in her teeth – it was a big, soft cushion, made of red fabric – and tugged it closer to the radiator. Then she nudged it with her nose, this way and that, as though she couldn't get it quite how she wanted it.

Lauren watched her hopefully. "Does that look like nesting to you?" she asked.

8

"I don't know. It might be..." her mum said doubtfully. It was the first time Bella had had puppies, and they were having to learn as they went along, even though Lauren's mum had bought three different books on dog breeding.

"We need to set off for school," Dad pointed out, checking his watch.

Lauren sighed. "I bet Bella has the puppies while I'm at school, and I really, really want to be there. Couldn't I just stay at home? It's the last day of term, we're not going to actually do anything, are we?"

Mum shook her head. "No. Besides, don't you want to say goodbye to all your friends? You won't see most of them for the next six weeks, remember."

Lauren frowned. It was true. She loved living way out in the country. Their home had been a farmhouse originally, and it had a huge garden. The old cowsheds had been made into her parents' office, and there was a barn across the yard that Lauren could play in. But there were bad things about it too. She lived twenty minutes' drive from the village where her school was, and her best friend Millie lived in a village that was about twenty minutes' beyond the school! So arranging to see Millie in the holidays always meant lots of planning.

Lauren fetched her bag and the present she'd got for her teacher, Miss Ford, and took one last look at Bella on the way out of the kitchen door. The beautiful brown and white dog was squirming around on her cushion as though she couldn't quite get comfy.

"Can you just hold on until I get home?" Lauren pleaded. But Bella looked up at her with big, mournful eyes. Lauren stroked her lovingly. "I see what you mean. You must really want to be back to your old self again. If it happens today, good luck, Bella. It'll be worth it, you're going to have gorgeous puppies soon."

"She's going to be very tired," Dad pointed out. "We'll have to look after her. I remember doing all this with Rusty, my parents' dog, when I was just a bit older than you. Now come on, Lauren, we're going to be late."

As they were bumping down the lane in the car towards the main road, Lauren asked, "How many puppies do you think Bella will have?"

Dad shook his head. "Hard to tell – could be anything from one to fourteen, according to those books your mum bought. Rusty only had five."

Lauren frowned. "It can't just be one. Bella's enormous."

"I think you're probably right – she is very big. I'd say we're looking at quite a few," Dad agreed.

He sighed as he noted her sparkling eyes and excited smile. "Lauren…"

"What is it?" Lauren looked over at him worriedly.

"Sweetheart, just remember that we aren't keeping these puppies. They're all going to go to new homes."

Lauren hesitated for a moment. "I know," she said quietly. She was silent for a little while and then added, "But we'll have them for a couple of months, won't we? That's all the summer holidays to play with them, and more."

Dad nodded. "Exactly. Of course we'll miss them when they go, but it'll be easier if we remember that they aren't ours to keep."

"I won't forget," Lauren promised. "Oh, there's Millie, Dad! Can you let me out here? I can walk up the road to school with her and her mum, can't I?"

Dad pulled up, and Lauren jumped out of the car, waving to her best friend.

"Hi! How's Bella? Have the puppies arrived yet?" Millie asked breathlessly.

Lauren shook her head, then smiled. "Bella was being really funny this morning. She kept messing around with her bed as if she was nesting. There might even be puppies when I get home!" she said, swinging her school bag excitedly.

"You're so lucky," said Millie. "Mum, can we have one of Bella's puppies? Pleeeease?"

"Oh, Millie, you know I'd love one," said her mum, hitching Millie's baby sister Amy higher up on her hip. "But it just wouldn't be fair to have a dog – I'm busy with your sister, and your dad's at work during the day. A puppy would get lonely."

Millie sighed. "I suppose so."

"You'll be able to play with them when you come round in the holidays," Lauren promised her. "And I won't get to keep the puppies either. Dad was reminding me in the car."

Millie nodded. "Still, you'll have weeks and weeks to play with them all. Oh, there's the bell. See you later, Mum!"

The two girls ran into class, and joined the crowd of children round Miss Ford, all begging her to open their goodbye present first.

Chapter Two

Lauren usually spent ages chatting to all her friends at the end of school, but today she was desperate to see if the puppies had arrived. She dashed out into the playground to find Dad waiting by the gate. Millie chased after her.

"Has Bella had the puppies yet?" Lauren gasped. She'd been running so fast she had to grab on to Dad's arm to stop herself falling over.

Dad steadied her, laughing. "Yes."

"How many?" Lauren squeaked excitedly.

Dad smiled. "Guess."

Lauren frowned. "Five?"

"Nowhere near. Ten!"

"Ten puppies?" Lauren turned round to Millie, her eyes round with amazement. "Ten? That's a *huge* litter!"

Millie laughed. "You'll have to think of ten names!"

"That's going to be tricky," Dad said. Lauren gave him a worried look. He didn't sound quite as happy as she thought the owner of ten puppies should. A sudden horrible thought hit her. Ten puppies was loads – it must have been such hard work for Bella, giving birth to so many. What if something was wrong with her? Lauren opened her mouth to ask, and then shut it again. She didn't want to talk about something so scary in the middle of the school playground.

Instead, she hugged Millie goodbye, and promised to email her a picture of the puppies later.

But as soon as she and Dad were heading for the car, she grabbed his hand. "Dad, is everything OK?"

"What do you mean?" Dad looked at her carefully.

"I just thought you seemed a bit worried — after you told us there were so many puppies. Is Bella all right?"

Dad gave her a hug. "Bella's fine. I mean, she's exhausted, but she did really well. It's not Bella..." He hesitated. "Lauren, one of the puppies is a lot smaller than the others. Mum and I — we're not sure this one will make it. It's such a tiny scrap of a thing, and when it was first born, we weren't even sure if it was breathing. Bella had another puppy straight after, and she didn't have time to lick the little puppy like she did with the others, or bite through its cord. I had to cut the cord myself, and I rubbed the little pup with a flannel to bring it round." He shook his head. "It did start to breathe, but it's not as strong as the other puppies, not by a long way."

"Do you think it might die, Dad?" Lauren whispered.

Dad sighed. "I hope not – but we have to face the fact that it might."

"That's so sad." Lauren felt tears stinging her eyes. The poor little puppy.

"Nine healthy puppies is a great litter," Dad reminded her.

Lauren nodded. "I guess so. But I can't help worrying about the little one."

"I know, me too. Still, it might perk up. You never know."

Lauren crossed her fingers behind her back. She wanted Bella to have all ten of her wonderful puppies safe and well.

Lauren crept in the kitchen door. She was trying very hard not to upset Bella.

But Bella looked like she'd be impossible to disturb. She was stretched flat out on her side, fast asleep on the pile of old towels that Mum had put aside for her and the puppies to sleep on, in the special low wooden pen Dad had made for them. They'd been worried that the puppies might fall off Bella's big cushion.

The puppies were all snuggled up next to their mum, fast asleep in a pile of heads and paws. Lauren knelt down beside the pen and tried to count them, but she couldn't work out where one pup ended and the next began.

She couldn't see which was the one that Dad was worried about, either.

"They're so tiny!" she whispered to Mum.

"I know, aren't they beautiful?" Mum beamed.

Lauren frowned. "They're all black and white! I can hardly see any brown on them at all. That's really weird, when Bella's brown and white."

Mum shook her head. "I thought that, but then I looked it up in our beagle book, and it says they're usually born mostly black and white. The black might change to brown over the next few weeks, or stay as it is. Most beagles are black and white with brown patches – tricolour, it's called. Bella's quite rare, being all brown and white."

"Look how pink their noses are," Lauren breathed. "And I can hear them snuffling! They're so gorgeous."

"Aren't they?" Dad agreed. "Oh, look, Bella's waking up."

Lauren watched Bella yawn and blink sleepily, and crouched closer to the pen, expecting Bella to want to lick her hand. She was such a friendly dog, and she loved to cuddle up with Lauren

– preferably on the sofa watching cartoons.

But today Bella seemed not to see her. She was only interested in her puppies. She nudged them awake, pushing them gently towards her tummy so they could start feeding.

"She was like that with me too," Mum murmured. "Not interested. It's as if she's only got eyes for her puppies now." She put her arm round Lauren's shoulders. "Don't worry. She'll only be like this for the first couple of weeks, until they open their eyes and start to move around. Then they won't need her so much, and she'll be our sweet Bella again."

Lauren nodded. "Can I pick up one of the puppies?" she asked. "Will Bella let us?"

"We haven't touched them yet," Dad said. "We didn't want to upset Bella."

Lauren peered at the pile of puppies, as Bella woke them up. "Which is the little one – the one that was having trouble breathing properly?" she asked anxiously. "Oh! I think I can see – is it the one Bella's licking?"

Mum nodded. "Yes, that one's definitely a lot smaller than the others."

"Oh, look, you can see its little brown eyebrows!" Lauren said admiringly.

She edged closer to the pen, and Bella glanced up, as if to check that she wasn't going to harm the puppies. Lauren shuffled back a little, and Bella quickly went back to licking and nudging at the tiny puppy. The others were all feeding already – Lauren could hear the strange, wheezy squeak as they sucked. She giggled. "Look, Mum, that puppy's sitting on the other one's head!"

Mum smiled. "I don't think they mind as long as they're getting their mum's milk."

Dad was looking at one of the others. "Hey, pup. I don't think that's going to do you much good," he chuckled. "Look, that big puppy's trying to suck Bella's paw."

Bella looked round at the sound of Dad's voice, and spotted the confused puppy. She wrinkled her nose, and then gently pushed the puppy over to her tummy to feed with its brothers and sisters. Then she went back to trying to rouse the tiny pup.

"That one really is loads smaller than

the others," Lauren said worriedly.

"And it's going to stay that way if it doesn't feed," Dad put in. "Oh, hang on though, look. Bella's got it moving."

The littlest puppy scrabbled wearily, its paws waving. It was making sad squeaking sounds, as though it wished Bella had left it to sleep, but at last it managed to burrow in among the rest of the litter.

"Is it feeding?" Mum asked hopefully.

"I think so." Lauren tried to listen for sucking sounds, but it was hard to tell with nine other puppies feeding at the same time. "Its head's moving backwards and forwards, like the others."

Dad nodded. "That's good, I was getting worried."

Then Lauren winced as one of the

other puppies kicked the tiny one in the stomach – not on purpose, the bigger puppy was just scrambling to get back to Bella's milk. The tiny puppy lay there, kicking feebly, and then it seemed to go back to sleep. Lauren watched anxiously, willing it to wake up and feed again. But the littlest puppy just lay where it was, while its brothers and sisters wriggled and kicked for the best spot.

Chapter Three

Hi Millie,

Here's a photo of the newborn puppies! I bet you can't count all ten in this picture, though, they're all squeezed up together. They're really gorgeous, but there's one tiny one that won't feed properly from Bella. I just hope it's going to get better. Please come and see the puppies soon.

Love Lauren x

Lauren sent her email to Millie, and went downstairs to find Dad making the dinner and Mum cuddling one of the puppies, while Bella sat at the edge of the pen and kept a close eye on her.

"Oh, wow, she let you pick one up!"

Mum nodded. "But I was very careful. I washed my hands, and then I stroked Bella first, so that I didn't make the puppy smell like me. The book I was reading said that it was good to start handling puppies early, to get them used to people, but I don't want to worry Bella. She doesn't seem too bothered, though – we thought she would be OK, as she's such a friendly dog." Mum ran her finger very gently down the snoozing puppy's back. "If you wash your hands, you can stroke the puppy, too."

Lauren carefully washed her hands, and made a fuss of Bella first, stroking her with both hands to get Bella's scent on her fingers. Then she stroked the puppy with one finger, like her mum had done. It felt like slightly damp velvet – and it was no bigger than one of the Beanie toy dogs she had on her windowsill upstairs. "It's so soft…" she breathed.

Bella made a little snorting noise, and lay down next to her puppies again, but she was still eyeing Lauren and her mum.

"Look how fat its tummy is," Mum pointed out. "This puppy's absolutely stuffed."

"I think we should put it back," Lauren said. "Bella looks a bit worried. But she hasn't growled or anything. She's such a good dog."

"And a good mother too," Dad said, from over by the cooker. "She's taken to it so well."

Lauren's mum gently slipped the puppy back into the pen next to Bella, who licked it all over. The puppy made a squeaking noise as Bella's big tongue licked its head, but it didn't wake up.

"Where's the tiny one?" Lauren asked, trying to count the puppies.

Mum frowned. "I'm sure I saw it just a moment ago, and I think it had some more milk, which is really good. Apparently Bella's milk is full of all sorts of good stuff on the day they're born. The puppies get all the benefit of the vaccinations she's had, that kind of thing."

"I can't see the little puppy now," Lauren muttered anxiously. "What if it's under all the others and they squash it?"

Mum knelt down next to her. "Isn't that it?" she asked, pointing to a puppy.

Lauren shook her head. "No, brown eyebrows, remember? That one's just black and white."

"Oh yes." Mum edged round to the other side of the pen. "It's here, look, behind Bella. It must have got pushed out of the way by the others."

Lauren followed her, moving slowly so as not to disturb Bella. "Is it OK?"

Bella was watching carefully, and as soon as she realized what had happened, she wriggled round and tried to nudge the puppy over with her nose. But the puppy was fast asleep and didn't move. Bella glanced up at Lauren and her mum, almost as though she wasn't quite sure what to do.

"Should we move the puppy for her?" Lauren asked, frowning.

Mum was starting to say, "Maybe we should…" when Bella leaned down and picked up the tiny puppy in her mouth.

"Mum, what's Bella doing?" Lauren whispered in horror.

"Don't worry," Mum soothed her. "It's fine. Dogs do that, Lauren, she won't hurt the puppy."

But it didn't look at all comfortable. The puppy's legs dangled out on either side of Bella's mouth, and it wheezed and squeaked unhappily. Bella swiftly tucked it in along the row of teats on her tummy, and watched hopefully.

Lauren and Mum watched too, and Dad left the pasta sauce he was stirring and came to peer over their shoulders, holding a tomatoey wooden spoon.

"It's feeding," Lauren whispered excitedly, seeing the little shoulders moving.

Mum nodded. "And as all the others are asleep, hopefully it'll be able to keep feeding for a while."

"Oh, that's good." Dad sighed with relief. "And good timing. Dinner's ready."

Lauren went to bed that night very reluctantly. She wanted to stay and watch the puppies, especially the tiniest one. She was still worried that it wasn't getting enough milk. Because it wasn't as big as the others, it couldn't wriggle its way back to Bella's teats when it got pushed away, like the others could. Instead of barging past its brothers and sisters, the littlest puppy would just whine miserably and go back to sleep.

"Can't I stay up a bit longer? It's the first day of the holidays tomorrow," Lauren begged.

"It's already an hour later than bedtime!" Mum pointed out. "You can come down early in the morning to see them. But now you need to go to bed."

Lauren sighed, recognizing Mum's no-argument voice. Still, she was sure she wouldn't ever sleep.

Lauren woke up suddenly, to find her bedroom in darkness. So she had fallen asleep after all.

She sat up, hugging her knees. What time was it? It felt like the middle of the night. She glanced at her luminous clock. Two o'clock in the morning. Lauren shuddered. No wonder it was so dark. She lay down again, but she didn't feel sleepy any more. Something was worrying her, and she wasn't sure what it was. Then she realized – the puppies! Of course, how could she have forgotten about them?

She couldn't hear any noise from downstairs. Bella and the puppies were probably fast asleep. But she couldn't stop worrying that something was wrong, and that was why she had woken up.

It wouldn't hurt to go and have a look, would it? Lauren smiled to herself – Mum had said she could come down early to see the puppies, after all. She probably hadn't meant quite this early, but still…

She got out of bed and crept over to her door, quickly pulling on her dressing gown. As she ran across the landing to the stairs, she could hear her dad snoring. She hurried down the stairs, and into the kitchen. She could make out little squeaks and sucking noises – the puppies were awake and feeding, but that wasn't really surprising. Lauren had been reading Mum's puppy books, and it said that for the first couple of weeks they would need to feed every two hours.

Mum had left a small lamp from the living room plugged in on the counter, so Bella had a bit of light for feeding the puppies. Bella was lying on her side looking sleepy, but she thumped her tail gently on the floor of the pen as she saw Lauren.

"Hey, Bella. I just came to see how you all are," Lauren whispered, kneeling beside the pen.

Bella closed her eyes wearily, as Lauren patted her head and leaned over to count the puppies. Then she counted them again. Only nine!

Where was the little puppy with the brown eyebrows?

"Oh, Bella, where's it gone?" Lauren whispered, but Bella was half-asleep, and she only twitched her tail.

Lauren checked behind Bella, where the puppy had ended up before, but there was nothing there. She was sure the other puppies weren't lying on the little one, and it couldn't possibly have climbed out. Frantically, Lauren started to feel around the shadowy edges of the box.

"Oh!" Lauren gasped, as she touched something little and soft, pushed away in the corner. "There you are!" She picked up the puppy, waiting for it to squeak and complain, but it didn't make a sound. "Oh, no, I didn't wash my hands – I suppose it's too late now." Lauren lifted the puppy up to see better, and realized that it was saggy and cold in her hands.

"Oh no, please…" she murmured, and snuggled the puppy in a fold of her dressing gown. "Mum! Dad!" she yelled, as she raced back up the stairs. "We need to call the vet!"

Chapter Four

"It woke up a little bit while I was holding it," Lauren explained to Mark, the vet. "Is it going to be all right?"

Mark put away his stethoscope and looked at the puppy thoughtfully. "You did really well to catch her when you did, Lauren. She's a she, by the way."

Lauren smiled, just a little. She had thought the puppy was a she – it was something about those cute brown eyebrows.

"It looks to me like she was slipping away," Mark went on, gently stroking the puppy's head. "Puppies can't control how warm or cold they are, they need their mum to keep them warm. You cuddling her warmed her up again. The real problem is that she's not strong enough to feed properly by herself. But you could hand-rear her." He glanced up at Lauren, and her mum and dad. "I can't promise she'll make it. But it's worth a try. It's a lot of work, though."

Lauren's dad frowned. "What does hand-rearing mean, exactly? I've looked after puppies before, but I've never had to hand-rear one. Would we feed her with a bottle?"

"A baby's bottle?" Lauren asked, looking at the tiny puppy. She was about the same size as a baby's bottle!

Mark shook his head. "No, a special puppy one. I've got one somewhere." He rooted about in his bag. "Here it is. I nipped into the surgery when you called and picked up some puppy milk replacement, and some advice on hand-rearing." He handed Lauren's dad a jar of white powder, and a leaflet. "You mix it with water, just like baby formula. Puppies can't drink cows' milk, it's got the wrong mix of nutrients."

Lauren's dad read the instructions on the jar. "Every two hours?" he asked, sounding slightly worried.

"Only for the first week," Mark reassured him. "After that you'll probably be able to leave her without a feed through the middle of the night."

Dad rubbed his eyes wearily – it was now four o'clock in the morning. He and Mum ran their own mail-order business from home, and he'd been up late checking orders. He nodded. "Well, that's what we'll do." He glanced at Mum, who was looking anxious. "We can't not," he added gently.

Mum nodded. "Of course. It's going to be hard though." She smiled at Lauren. "A bit like when you were little."

Mark smiled. "But puppies grow faster than babies. They stop drinking their mum's milk at about seven weeks old. This little one should be feeding herself before you know it."

Lauren nodded. If it worked… Mark hadn't sounded absolutely sure that it would. But Lauren had already saved this puppy once, and if it was anything to do with her, the little one was going to make it.

"I'll do it," she said to her parents. "The feeding, I mean. I don't mind."

"You can't get up every two hours in the middle of the night!" Mum said, sounding horrified.

Lauren went over to fill the kettle. "We should feed her now, shouldn't we? Do we have to use boiled water? Like Millie's mum uses for her little sister's bottles?"

Mark grinned at Lauren's parents. "It sounds like Lauren knows what she's doing."

Lauren beamed at him. She really wanted to help, but she had a feeling Mum and Dad weren't going to be keen. "Do we have to keep the puppy separate from the others?" she asked, trying hard to think of anything else they might need to know.

Mark frowned. "I would for tonight. She's obviously having trouble keeping warm, she'll need a box and a hot-water bottle. Look, the leaflet shows you.

But after tonight, she'd be better off staying with her mum and the rest of the puppies, if she can. Just take her out for her feeds. Best of luck, and if there's any problems, give the surgery a ring."

The boiled water took ages to cool down, and Lauren kept wanting to blow on it.

Mum went to prepare a box for Lucy, and Dad sat at the kitchen table reading the instruction leaflet Mark had left. "Small cardboard box. Blanket. Hot-water bottle," he muttered. "We should have thought about all of this before, but it just never crossed my mind that we'd have so many and Bella wouldn't be able to feed them all. Uuurrgh!"

"What?" Lauren turned round, still cradling the puppy.

Dad was making a face. "According to this leaflet, we're going to have to help the puppy poo... They don't do it themselves, apparently, so because Bella won't be licking her after she's fed, we'll have to wipe round her bottom with wet cotton wool."

Lauren made a face back. That *was* a bit yucky. But it didn't put her off. She was going to do anything she had to, to keep the puppy going. Even if that meant making her poo.

"I think this water's cool enough to mix the formula now. Not long till you can have some milk, Lucy."

"Lucy?" Mum asked. "When did you name her?"

Lauren looked up. "I didn't even notice I had! But don't you think she looks like her name's Lucy?"

Mum nodded, but she was frowning, and Lauren bit her lip. She had a horrible feeling that Mum hadn't wanted her to name the tiny puppy in case she didn't make it.

Lauren carefully spooned the powder into the bottle, and mixed in the water. "Wake up, little one… Does it say how to hold her, Dad?"

Her dad skimmed through the instructions. "Flat, on her tummy, not on her back like a human baby. Here, look, on a towel." He laid a towel over Lauren's knees, and Lauren set Lucy down on her tummy. Her paws splayed out and she scrabbled a little and let out a tiny squeak, unsure what was going on.

"It's OK." Lauren picked up the bottle, and gently put it against Lucy's mouth.

"Squeeze the bottle a little," Mum suggested. "She doesn't know what it is. Let her taste a few drops of the milk."

All of a sudden Lucy started to suck eagerly, as she tasted the milk in her mouth. Her tiny pink paws, with their little transparent claws, pattered against Lauren's fingers, making her giggle. "Wow, she was ready for that."

Lucy only took five minutes to down the bottle.

"Goodness, should we give her some more?" Mum asked.

Lauren shook her head. "No, this is how much Mark said for now. The tub of powder says how much you give for what size of puppy over a whole day, and then you have to divide that up between the feeds." She gave a big yawn, and on her knee, Lucy did the same.

Mum laughed. "I think we should all go to bed. Especially if we have to be up at six-thirty to feed her again."

Lauren looked up at her mum hopefully. "Mum, my bedroom's lovely and warm, and if I have her box in there, I can keep an eye on her…"

"But we have to feed her so early. You don't want to get up at half-past six in the holidays!" Dad smiled.

"I do, I really do!" Lauren promised. "I was the one who woke up and found her, Dad. I really want to help."

Dad looked over at Lauren's mum. "What do you think, Annie?"

Mum sighed. "I suppose so. But only for tonight, Lauren. Tomorrow, when she's a bit stronger, Lucy can go back with Bella and the other puppies."

Lauren nodded eagerly and picked up the cardboard box. Inside, Lucy was snuggling up against the well-wrapped hot-water bottle. She looked happier than she had all day, Lauren thought. She padded back up the stairs, yawning uncontrollably. She set the box down next to her bed, and fell asleep listening to the minute wheezy breaths from inside the box.

It was really hard to get up when Dad came in at half-past six, but Lauren dragged herself out of bed, and carried Lucy's box downstairs to watch Dad make up her next feed. The trip downstairs hadn't disturbed Lucy at all, she noticed with a smile. The puppy was still snoozing peacefully next to the cooling hot-water bottle.

In the kitchen, Bella was out of the puppy pen looking hungry, and Lauren fed her while Dad boiled the kettle.

"Can I feed Lucy again?" Lauren begged, and Dad handed her the bottle.

"You might as well – you certainly seemed to have the knack earlier!"

Going downstairs might not have

woken Lucy, but the smell of the puppy formula certainly did, and she was gasping and squeaking with excitement as soon as Lauren held the bottle to her mouth.

After she'd cleaned Lucy up, Lauren took her over to Bella. She and Dad hovered anxiously, not too close to the puppy pen, watching to see how Bella would react.

"I hope Lucy will be all right," Lauren muttered. "It said in that leaflet that sometimes the mum tries to lick the human smell away and accidentally hurts the puppy."

Dad put an arm round her shoulders. "We'll watch really carefully," he promised. "And it's not as if Bella's a dog at a big breeder's, who lives outside and doesn't really know people that well. She's part of our family. Hopefully our smell won't upset her too much."

"Look!" Lauren whispered.

Bella was sniffing thoughtfully at Lucy, and Lauren held her breath as Bella started to lick the little puppy. But Bella didn't look at all upset, just a little surprised.

Lauren giggled. "I think Bella's so worn out I bet she'd hardly noticed Lucy was gone!"

Over the next few days, Lauren was sure that Lucy had started to recognize her. If Lucy started squeaking in her box, she would calm down as soon as Lauren picked her up, but not if it was Mum or Dad. Lauren knew it was probably just that Lucy recognized her by smell as the person who usually fed her, but it still made her feel special. She couldn't wait for Lucy to open her eyes, so that the puppy could see her as well as smell her.

Mum and Dad were supposed to be taking it in turns to do the night feeds, but Lauren couldn't help waking up when she heard the alarm go off in their bedroom. And once she was awake, she just couldn't stay in bed. Mum even stopped telling her off about it by the end of their second night of puppy-rearing.

Lucy was putting on weight now,

although not as fast as the other puppies, who were fat and glossy-furred. She adored her feeds, but Lauren suspected she might always be a bit smaller than her brothers and sisters.

Lucy squeaked and sucked at Lauren's fingers as Lauren scooped her up. She knew Lauren's scent, and she was sure it was time for Lauren to feed her, and she was so, so hungry.

Lauren giggled as Lucy's little pink paws flailed around. "I'm just waiting for it to cool down. You don't want to burn your mouth!"

Lucy squeaked even louder. Where was the milk?

"OK, OK, here you go."

Lucy sighed happily, and settled down to sucking. That was much better.

After the first week, Lauren and her parents could leave Lucy for six hours in the middle of the night without a feed. Dad said he'd do the midnight feed on his own – he was used to staying up late working anyway. Lauren had to admit it was really nice to get a proper night's sleep again, even though she still had to get up super-early for Lucy's morning feed.

Millie came to visit the puppies when they were about two weeks old.

"Can I feed Lucy?" she asked hopefully. "That photo you sent me of you feeding her was so cute. She's even more gorgeous now her eyes are open, though."

"She is, isn't she?" Lauren agreed, handing Millie the bottle.

Lucy watched Lauren the whole time she was feeding, and Lauren could tell she was a bit confused why somebody else was holding her bottle.

"You have to burp her now, like your mum burps Amy!" Lauren told Millie, when Lucy had finished.

Now that the puppies were two weeks old, their eyes were open, although they still hadn't really started to move around much. The really exciting thing was that their markings were starting to come through. Lucy had more brown on her face now, not just her pretty eyebrows, and all the puppies were changing every day.

Even though the puppies were still too tiny to really play with, Millie didn't want to leave when her mum came to pick her up.

Lauren waved goodbye from the door, and sighed as Millie's car disappeared down the lane. She really missed seeing her best friend every day.

"Lauren, I've got some really exciting news," her mum started, as she came back into the kitchen. "Hey, what's the matter?"

"I just wish I could see Millie more often in the holidays, that's all. Email and phoning aren't the same as having a friend close by."

Her mum gave her a hug. "This is going to be extra-good news for you, then." She beamed at Lauren. "We've rented out the cottage. To a family with a boy the same age as you!"

Lauren blinked. The cottage was

on the other side of the orchard, just beyond the farmyard. The old tenant had left ages ago, and Lauren had forgotten they were trying to find someone new.

"He's called Sam Martin, and he's got a little sister called Molly. Isn't that wonderful? You'll have a friend really close by!"

Lauren nodded slowly, but she wasn't sure it was all that wonderful. What if she didn't like this boy? And even if she did, he wouldn't be as good a friend as Millie.

Chapter Five

"Oh, that sounds like the Martins at the door!" Mum fussed around the kitchen, putting the kettle on. "Would you open it, Lauren?"

It was two weeks after Mum had broken the news about the new neighbours moving in, and they'd said they were going to pop round that afternoon. Lauren still couldn't help wishing it was a girl her age rather than a boy. And she didn't want some strange boy and his little sister messing around with Lucy and upsetting her. Instead of opening the door, she quickly dashed upstairs with Lucy, and stashed her in the box she'd slept in on the first night. Mum still let her take Lucy upstairs occasionally, and Lucy couldn't get out of the box yet, although she really liked trying.

Lucy whined in surprise as Lauren put her down. What was happening? She had been having a nice cuddle, and now she was being left all on her own! She stood up with her paws against the edge of the box, scrabbling hard. Where was Lauren? She whimpered miserably.

Lauren ran back downstairs, and tried to look friendly as Mum introduced her to Nicky Martin and Sam, a blond-haired boy who looked just as embarrassed as she felt. Sam's dad was still sorting things out at the house, and his little sister was asleep, Nicky said.

Sam cuddled one of the puppies, the big boy that they had named Buster, and didn't really say much. Lauren was just hoping that they might go soon – surely they must have loads of unpacking to do? But then her mum nudged her, and said meaningfully, "Why don't you show Sam round the farm?"

Lauren frowned. It was nearly time to feed Lucy, and she didn't want to anyway!

Her mum glared at her, and she gave a tiny sigh and turned to Sam. "Come on, then. You can bring Buster, if you like."

Sam nodded, and followed her out into the yard. "He's really nice. Is he your favourite?"

Lauren shook her head.

"Don't you have a favourite? He'd be mine, he's great." Sam snuggled Buster up under his chin.

Lauren didn't know what to say.

It would sound stupid to admit she'd hidden Lucy away. "I like them all," she said, a bit vaguely.

Lauren trailed around the farm, showing Sam the orchard, and the old barn on the other side of the yard. There were a few bales of hay in it still, and she liked to hide out in there sometimes.

"This is cool. I bet the puppies would love it in here," said Sam.

Lauren nodded. "They haven't been outside much yet, but Dad's making a wire run so they can play in the orchard."

Sam looked up. "Oh, that's my mum calling. I suppose we have to go and unpack."

He handed Buster to Lauren, and they headed back to the farmhouse. Lauren supposed Sam was OK really – at least he liked the puppies – but she didn't think they were going to be best friends or anything, which was obviously what Mum was hoping.

"He was nice, wasn't he?" Mum asked, as they waved goodbye to Sam and his mum. "Gosh, look at Buster!" She tickled the puppy under the chin. "He's huge. I must see about putting an ad in the local paper about new homes for the puppies. And there are a couple of good puppy websites too."

Lauren swallowed. Her heart seemed to have suddenly jumped into her throat. New homes! She had almost forgotten about that – she had wanted to forget.

"But they're only a month old, Mum!" she cried.

"I know. But puppies go to their new owners at about eight weeks, and people don't just turn up and take a puppy home. We'll have to let them come and see the puppies – and we need to meet them to make sure we like them." She hugged Lauren. "We're not going to give Bella's lovely pups to just anyone, sweetheart, don't worry."

Lauren nodded. "But – but not Lucy?" she asked quickly. "She isn't big enough yet, Mum."

Mum nodded thoughtfully. "You're probably right. Lucy will have to be a bit older than the others when she goes. Not much though, I shouldn't think. You've done so well feeding her, she's catching them up." She looked at Lauren. "I know you really love Lucy, and it'll be hard for you to say goodbye, but you'll still have Bella, remember."

Lauren buried her nose in Buster's soft fur. She loved Bella, of course she did. But Lucy would have died if Lauren hadn't woken up that first night. It felt like she and Lucy belonged together. But Lauren just didn't think she could explain that to Mum.

She put Buster back in the puppy pen, and ran upstairs to fetch Lucy. When she opened her bedroom door, Lucy scrabbled at the side of the box with her claws, squeaking frantically.

"Oh, I'm sorry. I went off and left you, didn't I?" Lauren scooped up the puppy, her eyes filling with tears. "I didn't mean to." She sighed, feeling Lucy wriggle and squirm against her neck. "I don't ever want to leave you. But I'm not going to, am I? You're going to leave me. Oh, Lucy, I don't want you to go!"

The summer holidays seemed to have gone by so quickly, Lauren thought. She could hardly believe there was less than a week to go until school started! She supposed it was because she'd been busy all the time looking after Lucy and Bella, and the other puppies.

Lucy's brothers and sisters loved the little outdoor run that Lauren's dad had made for them, and spent lots of time out there now. Lauren's mum had put a photo of them all romping about on the grass on the pet website where she was advertising them to new owners.

Lauren wasn't sure about letting Lucy go out in the run yet – she was still so much littler than the other puppies, and Lauren was worried that they might hurt her with their rough and tumble games.

"Mum, can I take Lucy out to play in the orchard, if I'm really careful not to let her run off?"

Her mum put down the phone. "Yes, that's fine. Although I'm sure she'd be all right in the run with the others, you know. She's a lot bigger now."

Lauren sighed. She supposed Lucy was catching up. But she still wouldn't feed from Bella like they did. Dad said she liked her special bottles too much. They wouldn't have to do the bottle feeds for too much longer, though. Now that the puppies were five weeks old, they were all having solid food too. Lauren loved to watch them all eating. The first few meals had gone everywhere but into the puppies' mouths, and Bella had ended up having most of it as she'd licked it off the puppies. They had the same dry food as Bella, but mixed with the puppy milk Lucy had, and they always ended up with mush caked all over their ears.

"Who was on the phone?" Lauren asked, as she finished her toast. "It wasn't someone about the puppies, was it?"

"No, it was just Nicky, Sam's mum. We'd talked about sharing the school run next week, and she wanted to know if we'd rather do morning or afternoon. I said we'd pick you up in the afternoon, is that OK? I like hearing about your day."

Lauren gaped at her. "Sam's going to my school?" she asked.

"Well, of course he is. Yours is the only school close by."

"He's not in my class, is he?"

"No, he's in the other class in your year." Her mum frowned. "His mum and I talked about it when they came round, didn't you hear us?"

Lauren shook her head. She supposed she'd been too busy being grumpy about having to entertain Sam. And now she had to share lifts to school with him! She knew it would make less work for Mum and Dad, but she didn't want to share her car journeys; she liked having the time to chat to them.

Crossly, she picked up Lucy and

a ball from the puppy pen and stomped out into the yard.

Lucy squirmed excitedly in Lauren's arms, sniffing all the interesting new smells. She'd been everywhere in the house with Lauren, but this was different. A butterfly fluttered past, and she yapped at it in delight. When they got to the orchard, which had a brick wall all round it, Lauren gently put her down on the grass.

Lucy looked up at her, not sure what she was supposed to do. She gave an enquiring little whine.

"Go play!" Lauren rolled the ball, and Lucy chased after it, yapping. She tried to sink her teeth into it, but it was just too big, and she ended up rolling over on top of the ball with a squeak of dismay.

Lucy bounced up and went off sniffing around in the grass, until she came to a dock plant, with big shield-shaped leaves. She licked a leaf thoughtfully, and then seized it in her teeth, pulling hard. It sprang back, and she jumped around yapping fiercely, until Lauren nearly choked with laughter.

All of a sudden there was a heavy thud, and a big football bounced over the orchard wall and thumped on to the grass right next to Lucy, who whimpered in fright. She scampered over to Lauren.

Lauren snatched Lucy up in one arm, grabbed the ball with the other and ran across to the wall, to find Sam peering over it.

"Hey! You almost hit Lucy with that! What are you doing?" Lauren snapped.

"Sorry! I was just kicking the ball around…" Sam looked guilty.

"You could have hurt her!" Lauren told him, as she shoved the ball into his hands.

"Sorry…" Sam muttered again, and he walked away with his shoulders hunched up.

Lauren almost felt sorry for telling him off, but then Lucy wriggled into her neck, whimpering, and Lauren felt cross all over again.

When school started the next week, Lauren had to share lifts with Sam, as her mum had arranged, but Lauren hardly talked to him. She didn't really know what to say, and Sam seemed shy of her. She supposed it was because of the way she'd told him off in the orchard.

It was great being back at school and seeing all her friends again, but she really missed Lucy and the other puppies.

"Are they big enough for new homes yet?" Millie asked, at break.

"Mum's got people coming to see them already, and they can leave Bella after next week, she says. People have already chosen six of them. Not Lucy, though, she's still too little." *Thank goodness*, she added silently. At the weekend, a family had come to see the puppies, and the little girl had picked up Lucy, saying she wanted her.

Lauren had felt sick watching. Luckily, Mum had seen her horrified face, and explained that Lucy was too little to go for a few more weeks. The family had chosen two girl puppies named Daisy and Danni instead. But afterwards Mum had sat down with Lauren and hugged her, and explained that she was going to have to let Lucy go sometime.

"You'll really miss her, won't you?" Millie said, putting her arm through Lauren's, and Lauren nodded.

"Couldn't you ask your mum and dad if you can keep her?" Millie suggested.

"I wish I could," Lauren whispered. "They've always said we can't, that we already have Bella. But I just can't bear to think of Lucy belonging to someone else."

Chapter Six

Lucy watched the strange boy cuddling Buster and wondered who he was. There were lots of other people in her kitchen too, but they all seemed friendly. Everyone who had come to the house over the last two weeks had wanted to stroke her and her brothers and sisters, and play with them. It was fun, but it was confusing too. She had a feeling that this boy was going to take Buster away. He had been before, and this time he had picked Buster up straight away, and Buster had wagged his tail and yipped happily, the way Lucy did when Lauren cuddled her.

If Buster went away with this boy, then she would be the only puppy left. Daisy and Danni had gone with a little girl the day before. The girl's mother had put them in a special box with a wire front, and Lauren had taken her out to see Daisy and Danni drive off in a car. Lauren had hugged her extra tight, and seemed really sad, although she'd cheered up and giggled when Lucy licked her ear.

Lucy missed rolling over and over with all the others, now that it was just her and Buster. She still had Lauren to play with, of course, and that was her favourite thing. But was she going to go somewhere too, like all her brothers and sisters? She didn't want to. She wanted to stay here with Lauren.

The boy snuggled Buster under his chin, and then turned to put him into a carrier like the one Daisy and Danni went away in. Lucy watched them go out into the yard, and then she looked around the puppy run, with its rumpled blankets and scattered toys, and howled a big beagle howl.

"Oh! Did Buster go today?" Lauren asked in surprise when she got home – she had been to Millie's house for tea.

"Yes, it's only Lucy left," her mum answered. "Did you have a good time?"

"Yes, it was great," Lauren replied, only half listening. She was looking at Lucy curled up asleep on the fluffy bed at one side of the puppy run. She seemed so tiny and alone.

Lucy woke up and stared around her at the empty run, looking confused. She let out a tiny whimper, and staggered to her feet, sniffing around the pen. Bella leaned over and licked her gently, and Lucy stopped whimpering, but she still looked uncertain.

Mum put her arm around Lauren. "She's got so much bigger, hasn't she? And you can really see all the brown coming out on her now. She's going to be so beautiful. You did really well with the hand-rearing, Lauren, it was such hard work. Dad and I are very proud of you, you know."

"Thanks," Lauren muttered. She was proud of what she'd managed with Lucy too, but she had a horrible feeling that she knew what was coming next.

"I know you'll miss her, sweetheart, but she's ready to go to a new home, isn't she?" Mum said gently. "She's hardly bothering with her bottles, and she's having dry food now."

Lauren nodded, and sniffed. It was all true, but that didn't make it any easier. She pulled away from her mum with a muttered, "Sorry!", picked up Lucy, who squeaked in surprise, and fled upstairs.

Lauren was really looking forward to Friday and the start of the weekend. She enjoyed being back at school, but she missed Lucy so much – and she wasn't sure how much more time they had together.

Her dad had picked up her and Sam as usual, and they sat in the back seat while Dad tried to ask cheerful questions about how Sam was settling in, and Sam kept saying things like, "OK," and, "Fine thanks."

They dropped Sam off, and then Lauren ran inside to say hello to Lucy.

The phone was ringing as she went into the kitchen, and her mum yelled from upstairs, "Can you answer that, Lauren? I'm just making the beds!"

Lauren grabbed the phone, hoping it wasn't an order for her parents' camping supplies company, as she always worried she'd get them wrong.

"Hello?"

"Is that Mrs Woods? With the beagle puppies?"

"Oh! Yes – I mean, I'm her daughter," Lauren explained.

"Oh good. Do you have any puppies left? I've only just seen the website."

Lauren swallowed. This lady might end up being Lucy's owner. All of a sudden her eyes filled with tears. "There is one puppy left," she said, making her voice sound very doubtful.

"Right – is there something wrong with it?" the lady on the phone sounded worried.

"We-ell… She was the smallest of the litter, you see, much smaller than the others. We had to hand-rear her."

"Oh dear. Well, if she's not healthy I think I'll try someone else. Thanks, anyway."

Lauren pressed the button to end the call with a shaky hand, and put down the phone.

But she couldn't answer the phone every time someone called…

Still feeling really guilty, Lauren took Lucy out into the garden to play. She threw a ball for Lucy to chase, and she raced up and down the garden with excited squeaks.

"Lauren!" Mum was calling from the little bit of garden round the side of the house, where the washing line was. "Can you help me hang the washing out, please?"

Lauren sighed. Hanging out the washing was one of the jobs she did to earn her allowance. "Sorry, Lucy," she said, picking her up. "You go in the run, OK? Back soon."

Lucy stared after her, whining. Lauren had left the ball on the grass, and there were no toys in the run. Lucy ran up and down, sniffing at the wire, then scratched at it, wondering if she could get out and fetch the ball. She stuck a small paw through the wire fence, but the ball was too far away to reach.

Yapping crossly, Lucy scratched at the wire again, standing up on her hind paws. Her claws caught in the wire. She looked at them thoughtfully, and unhooked them. Then she stretched up higher, clinging on tight. She was climbing! Wriggling and scrambling, she worked her way up the side of the run. She teetered on the top, not quite sure what to do next. All at once, she let go and scrambled down the other side, landing in a little heap.

She sprang up and shook herself excitedly. There it was – her ball! She chased after it, scrabbling it along with her front paws, and followed the ball as it rolled through the garden gate, and out into the yard.

Ten minutes later, Lauren dashed back, eager to go on playing with Lucy, only to find that Lucy wasn't there.

She stood staring at the run. The fence was about thirty centimetres high – surely Lucy was far too little to climb out?

"Lucy! Lucy!" Lauren cried, as she ran all round the run.

But the little puppy was nowhere to be seen.

Chapter Seven

Lucy pattered across the yard, and set off exploring around the other side of the orchard wall. She'd abandoned the ball in favour of all the other interesting things she could smell. Perhaps she'd find Lauren if she went down here, too. She spotted a snail climbing up the wall and watched it round-eyed. She went closer and sniffed. It had an odd smell, and she decided it wasn't for eating.

"Hey! Lucy!" Lucy jumped, and looked up. That wasn't Lauren's voice.

It was the boy, Sam, holding a big ball. She'd seen him before when he came to the house to fetch Lauren in the mornings. She sniffed his fingers in a friendly sort of way. Maybe he would play with her?

"Are you supposed to be out here on your own?" he asked. "I bet you're not."

"Lucy! Lucy!" There was a distant voice calling, sounding worried.

"You're definitely not," Sam told Lucy. "That sounds like Lauren looking for you."

Lucy could hear Lauren too, but she wasn't quite sure where she was. She whimpered anxiously.

"It's OK. Let's find Lauren, yes?" Sam looked down at her, and Lucy pawed his foot eagerly.

"Come on then. Good girl," Sam put down the ball, and picked up Lucy. He walked quickly down to the yard. "Hey, Lauren, I've got her!"

Lauren came dashing out of the garden gate. She grabbed Lucy, hugging her tightly while Lucy whined with delight. "Oh, you star, Sam! I was really worried. She must have climbed out of her run. Thanks!"

"Beagles are really good at escaping." Sam nodded, and Lauren looked at him in surprise. "I really like dogs," he explained. "We can't have one, because Dad's allergic, but I've got loads of dog books. And I once saw a video on a website of a beagle climbing out of a massive pen."

"Oh." Lauren suddenly felt really ashamed. She'd been going to school with Sam every day, and she hadn't asked him anything about himself, or said a single friendly thing. "It's brilliant that you found her. What if she'd gone on to the road?"

Sam nodded. "I can't imagine losing a dog like that," he agreed. "It would be awful."

Lauren's eyes suddenly welled up.

"Sorry! I didn't mean to make you cry!" Sam said, looking horrified.

"It's OK," Lauren gulped. "It's just – you don't understand…" She wiped her hand across her eyes, while Lucy licked at her cheek anxiously.

"Lucy isn't mine. Not for ever. She's going to have a new home, just like the other puppies. And I can't bear the thought of not having her any more."

"Oh wow," Sam muttered. "I thought you were keeping her, when she stayed and all the others went. And she's with you all the time."

"I've always known she'd have to go, like her brothers and sisters," Lauren whispered. "I still have Bella, and of course I love her, but I've spent so much time with Lucy, because we hand-reared her. It's going to be awful when she leaves. It was bad enough when people came for the others, but Lucy's special." She opened the orchard gate, and gently shooed Lucy in. "Want to come and play with her?" she said.

Sam nodded and followed her. "Has anyone come to see Lucy?" he asked.

Lauren shook her head. "Someone rang earlier, and I sort of mentioned how Lucy was the runt of the litter and made this lady think she wasn't very well…"

She glanced at Sam, not sure what he'd think, but Sam looked impressed.

"I felt really guilty afterwards," Lauren admitted. "And I can't keep putting people off."

Sam looked thoughtful. "There must be something you can do. I'll help you." He looked at Lucy, who was destroying a windfall apple. "You can't lose her," he said firmly.

Lauren smiled. He sounded so certain it made her feel a little bit better.

The next morning, Sam knocked at the kitchen door while Lauren was finishing her breakfast, and slipping cornflakes to Bella and Lucy, who were sitting on either side of her chair.

"Morning, Mrs Woods," he said politely to Lauren's mum. "Um, I was just wondering if Lauren wanted to come out and play."

"I'm sure she does!" Lauren's mum said, looking delighted, and Lauren rolled her eyes at Sam, who tried not to laugh.

"I'm popular then," he said quietly, as they went across the yard with Lucy and Bella on their leads.

"Mum thinks it's really nice for me

to have a friend living close by." Lauren swallowed nervously. "Sorry I haven't been very friendly. I was a bit cross when Mum arranged the lifts and everything – like I didn't have a choice."

"Me too!" Sam agreed. "My mum kept going on about how lucky I was, and I was like, she's a girl and I've never even met her! Sorry," he added. "Anyway, I've got a plan!"

"You have?" Lauren asked eagerly. "Tell me."

Sam sat down on the rusty old tractor that had been abandoned on the edge of the field and beamed. "I think we should buy Lucy ourselves! I've got thirty pounds of birthday money left. I'd give you that, no problem, if I could sort of share Lucy. Take her for walks sometimes and stuff. It's the closest I'll get to having a dog, after all."

Lauren nodded slowly. "I've got the money my gran gave me at the beginning of the holidays, but I've been so busy with the puppies I never got round to spending it. That's fifty pounds so far. Puppies can't cost more than a hundred pounds, can they? But how are we going to find the rest of the money?"

Sam grinned. "I thought we could pick the apples from the orchard, and sell them. We could set up a stall on that big patch of grass where the lane down to the farm ends. It's close enough to the road for people to see us and stop."

Lauren jumped off the tractor wheel. "That's a brilliant idea! Mum and Dad never have time to pick them, they won't mind. I'll go and get some buckets."

It took a while to pick the apples, as a lot of them had wasps in, and had to be thrown on the compost heap, but eventually they had three buckets of really nice-looking ones. Lauren grabbed a handful of freezer bags from the kitchen, when they went back home for lunch, and Sam found an old folding table in the big shed at the back of the cottage, and he borrowed one of the boxes from the move to make into cardboard signs.

Then Lauren had another brainwave. "You start selling the apples. I've just remembered, Mum's always saying I ought to clear out my old soft toys. We can sell those, too. Here, you take

Lucy, I'm going to sneak back home and get them."

By the time she struggled down the lane with a bin bag full of bears and dogs, Sam was looking very pleased with himself. "I've sold three bags! That's one pound fifty!" He'd made the signs as well, and tied a couple on to the hedges on both sides of the road.

apples
50p

"Brilliant! Help me put out the toys on the grass at the front of the table. They're bound to make people look."

"Lucy and Bella have been making people stop too, they've had loads of petting."

It turned out the toys were almost more popular than the apples. Lauren even had to go back and find some more soft toys that she hadn't been planning to get rid of, but she didn't mind giving up her Beanie toy dogs if it meant she could keep her real one.

"How much have we made?" Sam asked, as they packed up at teatime.

"Twenty pounds!" Lauren beamed. "So that's seventy altogether. And there's loads more apples we can pick. But I don't think I've got any more old toys."

Lauren's mum and dad were so pleased she was getting on with Sam that they didn't ask what they'd been doing all afternoon. And they didn't mind at all when she and Sam and the dogs disappeared off again the next morning.

It was the middle of the morning, and they were doing quite well, when a car pulled up by the stall.

"Would you like some apples?" Sam asked, sounding very professional, and the man smiled and dug around in his pockets for some change.

"Actually, I'm looking for Redhills Farm," he explained, as Lauren handed the apples through the car window.

"It's down there." Lauren pointed down the lane.

"Thanks. I've come to look at a beagle puppy – is that the mum? She's beautiful." He nodded at Bella, who was sitting by Lauren's side. He couldn't see Lucy, as she was curled up asleep, half inside Sam's hoodie top.

"Y-yes…" Lauren stammered, and the man waved and drove away.

Sam and Lauren stared at each other in horror. The man had come about Lucy! They were too late!

Chapter Eight

"What are we going to do?" Lauren whispered. "We can't let him have her, we can't! Mum didn't say anyone was coming, he must have just turned up."

Sam nodded. "We've nearly got enough money, as well. It's not fair."

Lauren looked at him, frowning. "If Lucy's not there, he can't see if he likes her..." she suggested slowly.

"You mean we should stay here?" Sam asked.

Lauren shook her head. "No. Because he's seen us, and Mum knows we've got Lucy. We have to hide. Come on!"

"Where are we going?" Sam asked.

"I don't know yet. Let's just get away from here."

"OK." Sam zipped up his hoodie, and used it like a bag to carry Lucy, while Lauren grabbed Bella's lead.

Lucy woke up as they ran back down the lane, as Sam was jiggling her around inside his top. She gave an indignant squeak, and tried to wriggle out.

Lauren turned back. "I'll take her, she'll be quieter with me. Shhh, Lucy!" Lucy snuggled gratefully into Lauren's arms, as Sam handed her over.

As they peered round the corner of the barn, they saw the man's car parked in the yard. The top half of the back door was open and they could see him talking to Lauren's mum in the kitchen.

"Let's hide in the barn," Lauren said quickly. "If we go behind the bales of straw, we'll still be able to see if they come out."

They sneaked through the open doors, and settled themselves at the back of the barn.

"Shhh! I can hear my mum," Lauren whispered.

"Lauren! Lauren!" They could just see Lauren's mum, looking a bit embarrassed. "She's probably in the orchard, playing with Lucy," she said.

"I'm sorry, I should've called first," the man said. "I saw the ad and thought I'd just drop in, as I was coming this way. There were two children up at the top of the lane with a beagle."

"Oh! Well, that would be Lauren and Sam. I hope they haven't gone along the road, Lauren knows not to. I'd better go up there and find them. You stay here and drink your tea."

Lauren sank back behind the straw bales. "She's going to be upset when she finds we aren't there," she said slowly.

"Do you want to let your mum know where we are?" Sam asked.

Lauren chewed her lip uncertainly, but then Lucy woke up again inside Sam's hoodie and wriggled out. She gave a little yap, and looked up at Lauren with her big brown eyes. She looked so gorgeous that Lauren knew she couldn't bear to let her go. "No," she said firmly. "He'll give up waiting soon, hopefully."

Lucy climbed off Lauren's lap and went sniffing round the floor, and nudging up against Bella, who was sensibly curled up on a pile of straw. Bella yawned and licked Lucy half-heartedly. It looked like she just wanted to sleep.

Lucy could smell delicious smells all

round the barn. She pattered off round the edge of the bale to investigate, and Lauren and Sam both dived to grab her, which made Bella bark.

"Ssshhh!" Lauren hissed, putting her finger to her lips, and Bella gave her a confused look. "Sorry, Bella, sweetie. But we have to be quiet, OK?"

Sam put Lucy in his lap, and started to wave a piece of straw for her to chase. "I don't think we can keep this little one quiet, though," he said, as Lucy squeaked delightedly and growled at the straw.

"They might not hear from out there. Oh, there's Mum. She looks a bit worried," Lauren said guiltily.

Lauren's mum went into the house, and obviously told the man she couldn't find Lauren and Lucy, because he came out and got into his car.

"I'm so sorry," Lauren's mum said.

Lauren thought the man looked disappointed, but she was more worried about the anxious look on her mum's face.

The man handed Lauren's mum a bit of paper. "Here's my phone number, anyway. If you could give me a ring." Then he drove off down the lane.

Lucy growled at the straw again. Sam had stopped waving it about, and she was getting bored. She whined loudly, and tugged the hem of Lauren's jeans with her teeth. She wanted them to play properly.

"Should we come out, now he's gone?" Sam asked.

Lauren wanted to, especially as she could hear her mum calling for her dad, who was working in the office at the back of the house. Now they'd both be searching for her. But she shook her head. "What if they just call the man to come back?" She nibbled her nails. "I think we have to give it a bit longer."

They could hear Lauren's mum and dad going round the house shouting her name. Finally, Bella started whining. "I know, Bella," Lauren whispered. "I'm hungry too."

"I'm starving," Sam muttered, and then he gasped as he heard a different voice. "That's my mum!"

Sam's mum came running into the yard carrying Molly. Molly was crying and calling, "Sam?"

Sam and Lauren exchanged a guilty glance.

"I'm sorry, I'll have to go out. Molly looks really upset…" Sam was getting to his feet. "You stay, I'll say I wasn't with you."

"It's OK, I'm coming too," Lauren told him. "And I promise you won't get into trouble. I'll say it was all my idea." They crept over to the barn door, and peered out anxiously. Bella looked round their legs, unsure what was going on. Only Lucy was happy, and squeaked excitedly to see everyone.

"Sam!"

"Lauren!"

"Didn't you hear us calling you? We've been shouting for ages!" Lauren's mum hugged her. "We had no idea where you were!"

Molly struggled down from her mum's arms and ran to hug Sam.

"Were you in the barn the whole time?" Dad asked, looking from Lauren to Sam and back again.

"Um, yes…" Lauren admitted.

"So you were hiding on purpose," Dad said.

Lauren glanced worriedly at Sam, and then said, very fast, "That man had come to buy Lucy, and I didn't want him to."

Mum blinked. "He was very nice. He already has one beagle, and wanted another. He was really disappointed when we couldn't find you."

"Sam, I can't believe you frightened us all like that," his mum said crossly.

"I think we'd all better go inside," Dad said firmly. "I want to understand what's going on here." He shooed Sam and Lauren and the two dogs into the kitchen, where Bella and Lucy went eagerly to their food bowls. "Sit down, you two. Right. Explain. What was wrong with that man that made you decide to do something so silly? He seemed like he'd be a really good owner."

"Nothing…" Lauren began haltingly.

"It wasn't him," Sam put in. "We didn't want anyone to have Lucy. Look." He dug in his hoodie pocket and brought out the old pencil case he'd been keeping the money in.

"Eighty-four pounds," Lauren said proudly, as he emptied it on to the table.

Dad frowned. "I don't get it."

"We were going to buy Lucy ourselves!" Lauren explained. "I really, really don't want to sell her to some stranger! We thought a puppy probably costs about a hundred pounds, and we were so close to having it, and then that man came! We had to hide Lucy away in case he got her first!"

"Is this something to do with the table full of apples at the top of the lane?" Mum asked.

Lauren nodded. "We sold the apples from the orchard, and my old toys, too."

"And it's my birthday money."

"And my money from Grandma."

"There's more apples left," Sam added. "We should get to a hundred, easily."

Mum smiled sadly. "That man was going to pay four hundred pounds. That's what a pedigree puppy costs."

"Four hundred!" Lauren whispered in horror. "We couldn't raise that much. Oh no..." And she started to cry. She was going to have to give Lucy up after all.

Lucy looked up from her bowl. What

was the matter with Lauren? She dashed across the kitchen floor, and scrabbled frantically at Lauren's legs.

Lauren reached down and picked Lucy up, cuddling her close, while Sam stroked her head.

Lucy howled loudly, joining in with Lauren's sobbing.

"Lauren, shhh…" her dad said gently. "And please tell Lucy to hush too, I can't hear myself think. That's better," he added, as Lauren stroked Lucy and shushed her. "We didn't realize you were that desperate to keep Lucy. Why didn't you say?"

"I tried!" Lauren burst out. "But you kept saying we had Bella, and ever since the puppies came you'd said we couldn't keep them. I told Sam about it, didn't I?"

Sam nodded. "But we thought if we had enough money we could keep her. Lauren said I could share her too."

"Oh, Sam…" his mum said sadly. "He loves dogs," she explained to Lauren's parents. "But his dad is allergic."

Lauren's mum was watching Lucy, snuggling up in Lauren's arms, her eyes switching from person to person, as she tried to follow what was going on. "She is lovely," Mum said slowly.

Lauren's dad looked round at her. "It was you that said no more dogs, Annie!"

"Somehow I can't imagine being back to just one, after all those puppies. It already seems very quiet, with only Bella and Lucy." Mum smiled. "And she's definitely the prettiest of the litter."

"So can we keep her?" Lauren asked, not quite sure whether that was what her mum was saying. "Really? You mean it?"

Mum nodded, and laughed as Lauren hugged her, squidging Lucy in between them. "Don't squash her!"

"But if Bella has puppies again, we're not keeping any!" Dad said sternly.

Lauren shook her head. "Oh no, I promise I wouldn't even ask!"

"You can have your birthday money back, Sam," Lauren's mum said, smiling.

Sam nodded, but he looked a bit sad.

"Do you still want to share Lucy, though?" Lauren asked, holding Lucy out to him.

Sam nodded eagerly, and Lucy wagged her tail so fast it almost blurred, and then licked his hand lovingly.

"We can use the apple money to buy her a really smart new collar and lead," Lauren suggested. "Not Bella's old ones any more. And we can put 'This dog belongs to Lauren and Sam' on her collar tag."

Everyone laughed, and Lucy howled again, a real show-off howl with her ears thrown back and her tail wagging under Sam's arm.

Sam grinned. "I think she likes that idea.

Jess the Lonely Puppy

For Robin and William

Chapter One

Chloe laughed delightedly as the ducklings squabbled over the bread. It was probably a special treat for them, she decided, as it wasn't just any old bread, but the crusts of her cheese-and-ketchup sandwiches. Ducks probably didn't get ketchup very often. She crouched down by the edge of the lake to watch them. The ducklings polished off the last few crumbs, and then circled hopefully nearer, in case she had any more. They were so sweet – mostly brown, with yellow streaks and patches, and really fluffy. Their mother was paddling watchfully around them, eyeing Chloe carefully.

A couple of the little ducks were getting braver now, swimming closer and closer. Chloe held her breath as the pair of them clambered on to the muddy edge of the lake with awkward little hops. They were coming to see her! She just wished she had some more sandwich for them. The bravest of the ducklings pecked thoughtfully at the toe of her trainer, but didn't seem very impressed.

"Sorry," she whispered, trying not to

laugh out loud and scare them away. "I haven't got anything else!"

Suddenly there was a scuffling noise and an ear-splitting bark. A little black-and-white dog burst through a clump of reeds and nearly knocked Chloe into the lake.

The ducklings squeaked in alarm and leaped back into the water, swimming away as fast they could, little feet paddling furiously.

"Oops!" The boy chasing the dog grinned. "Sorry, Chlo, did Jess knock you over?"

"No, I'm just sitting in the mud because I feel like it!" she snapped. She looked out across the lake, watching the mother duck and her babies speeding off into the deeper water, away from badly behaved dogs. She wished she could swim away too.

Jess watched the ducklings and barked after them happily. She'd never seen ducklings before, and they were very exciting.

"Why isn't she on her lead?" Chloe asked her brother crossly, as she struggled to her feet and tried to brush the sticky mud off her denim shorts. "She's not old enough to walk on her own, Mum and Dad said. She might run off and get lost, or get into a fight with another dog."

Will shrugged. "There's no one else around, Chloe; why shouldn't she have a run? She isn't bothering anyone."

"She's bothering me," Chloe growled. She knew she sounded grumpy and miserable, but she had really been enjoying playing with the ducks, and she'd hoped the bravest one might even have let her stroke him.

Will sighed and rolled his eyes, and Jess, bored now that the ducks had disappeared, scrabbled her muddy paws up against Chloe's legs, hoping for some of the bread she could smell.

"Ow! Get her off me!" Chloe squeaked, dodging sideways and almost falling into the lake. Will grabbed her arm to pull her back, and Chloe shoved him away crossly. Jess jumped around them with ear-splitting barks, thinking that this was all a game.

"What's going on? Are you two all right? Chloe, come away from the edge, sweetheart, you might go in. And I'm not diving after you!"

Chloe and Will's grandad gently pulled them away from the water. Chloe had started crying, and Will looked cross. Jess whined. She wasn't sure what was going on, but suddenly she didn't like this game any more. She slunk away from the children, and trotted off round the side of the lake.

"Go and get her, Will," Grandad said. "Put her back on her lead. She isn't really old enough to go off the lead yet."

Will chased after Jess, who darted away, glad that this was a game again. Grandad put his arm round Chloe. "What's up? Jess didn't hurt you, did she?"

Chloe shook her head. "She just knocked me over and got me all muddy. But I was watching those ducks, and she chased them all away. Why does she have to be so rough?"

"She's only little, Chloe. Puppies are silly like that. And Jess doesn't know her own strength."

Chloe sniffed and looked over at Jess and Will, who were running back towards them now.

"Why don't you take her for a walk round the lake with Will, once he's got her back on the lead?" Grandad suggested gently. "I'll come too, if you want."

Chloe hesitated. She'd like to go, if Jess was on the lead... But then the puppy spotted two Canada geese flying overhead and barked at full volume, jumping up and trying to catch the birds, who ignored her completely.

She shrank back against Grandad. "No, it's OK. I'll go back and sit with Mum and Dad, and read my book."

Grandad sighed as he watched her run back to her parents, who were sitting on the picnic rug. He followed after her slowly.

Jess scampered off, and Will laughed as she pulled hard on her lead. She loved walks like this, with lots of different things to sniff out and chase. She caught sight of another duck in the distance and woofed happily, turning back to glance bright-eyed at Will. They raced away excitedly together.

Chloe sat down on the rug and stared at her book, but she wasn't really reading it. It was a book about a girl and her dog, which was quite funny really, she realized. Girls who read dog books were supposed to like dogs, not be scared of them.

Chloe propped her chin on her hands and reread the first line of the page, but she just couldn't concentrate. Why hadn't she gone with Grandad and Will to walk Jess? She had been so excited when Mum and Dad had finally given in and said yes, they could get a puppy at last. Will and Chloe had been begging them for ages. It was going to be a family dog, who belonged to everyone, even though it was Will who was the keenest. He was ten now, and Mum and Dad had said that if he was really careful he and Chloe would be able to take the puppy out on their own, once they'd been to some dog-training classes.

Unluckily, although the Greys had had Jess for six weeks now and she was big enough to go out for proper walks, the dog-training classes had clashed with Will's football practice, so Jess hadn't been to any yet. Will didn't mind too much. He and Dad took her for really long walks when Dad got home from work, or sometimes he went with Grandad.

But Chloe didn't go at all. She had been sure that everything would be OK.

She couldn't possibly be scared of a tiny little puppy, could she? When they'd had a family discussion to decide what sort of dog they should get, she had said she didn't mind as long as it was friendly and sweet, and not too big. And not a boxer.

It had been a boxer who'd frightened her three years ago, back in her first year at school. She'd been running after Mum and Will through the park on the way home, and she'd gone a bit too close to the big dog. It had thought she was going to snatch the stick it was playing with and snapped at her. The boxer hadn't really hurt Chloe, just torn her cardigan sleeve, but she had been terrified, and Mum had been furious with the dog's owner. She'd told the boy that his dog should be on a lead if it wasn't properly under control. She'd said she'd report him to the police if she ever saw it loose in the park again.

Then Mum had explained to Will and Chloe that they mustn't ever, ever go near strange dogs, even if they looked friendly. Chloe had known that already, of course, but she hadn't meant to upset the dog. She'd just run a little bit too close.

For ages, she would beg Mum to take them the long way home from school so they didn't have to go through the park, where there were always people walking dogs. But that had been three years ago. She could walk through the park now, although she wouldn't stroke even the friendliest dogs.

Chloe had been certain that a puppy would be all right. She loved the *idea* of having a dog, and a puppy that she knew from when it was tiny – surely she wouldn't be scared?

But it hadn't worked out like that at all. The first time Chloe had seen Jess, the Border collie puppy was gorgeous – so fluffy, like a little black-and-white ball. They had gone to see the litter of puppies at the breeder's, and Chloe and Will had laughed at the funny little pups climbing over each other and bouncing around their pen. Chloe had been so excited, and when she finally plucked up the courage to stroke the little black-and-white head, Jess had licked her hand with a tiny pink tongue.

Chloe had loved her all at once.

She could see Will and Jess now, playing by the tall trees at the edge of the lake, Jess jumping excitedly at the stick that Will was waving. It was the kind of energetic game Jess loved.

That was Chloe's problem. Jess wasn't just fluffy and sweet. She was jumpy too, and wriggly and loud. Will played with her all the time, and that made her even more excited. She would jump around his feet, barking away, and Chloe couldn't help looking at her sharp little white teeth. She'd been looking forward to the puppy curling up on her lap for a cuddle sometimes, but Jess just didn't seem to be that sort of dog.

Chloe tried to hide it, but even though she wanted to, she was too scared to touch her. And Jess had Will, who loved her so much. Why would she bother with a girl who never stroked her, and pulled away even if Jess just gave her an interested sniff?

Chapter Two

Chloe was half-reading, and half-listening to Grandad and her parents chatting, when a loud bark made her jump. She watched as the puppy suddenly appeared from among the trees, streaking towards them in a black-and-white blur.

"She's running about off her lead again," she said nervously.

Mum looked round at Jess. "She's just having fun, Chloe, don't worry."

Jess stopped a little way away from the picnic rug and barked again anxiously. She needed them to come now, but they were just staring at her. She pawed at Chloe's leg, but Chloe pulled away with a frightened squeak.

Jess shook her ears crossly. Why did Chloe always do that? Frantically, she ran back towards the trees a little way and barked again.

"I think something's wrong," Dad said, frowning and getting up. "Where's Will?"

Will! Yes, they'd understood at last! Jess whined again, and then wagged her tail as Dad and Chloe finally followed her. Will had told her to fetch them, and even though she hadn't wanted to leave him, she was desperate to help.

"Oh, no..." Dad muttered as they got closer to the trees. Huddled at the bottom of one of the taller trees was Will. Dad and Chloe broke into a run.

"It's all right, we're here now," Dad said, as he crouched down by Will.

"I fell – I got really high up and a branch broke..." Will said faintly.

"Don't worry, we'll sort you out,"
Dad said soothingly. He turned to
Chloe. "Go and get your mum and tell
her to phone an ambulance. I think
Will might have broken his leg."

Jess sat in the kitchen in her basket,
whimpering every so often. She didn't
know what was happening, but things
were definitely not right. And she didn't
know where Will was.

"Shh, shh, Jess," Grandad said gently,
stroking her head. "Don't worry. Poor
Jess, it must have been very frightening
for her, seeing Will like that."

"It was frightening for everybody,"
Chloe whispered, cupping her hands

round her hot chocolate. Grandad had made it for her. He said even though it was summer, there was nothing like hot chocolate when people were upset. But it didn't seem to be working.

"I wish Mum would ring." Chloe stared hopefully at the phone, as though that would make it burst into life. "She promised she'd ring as soon as she knew what was happening."

Grandad patted Chloe's hand, a bit like he'd stroked Jess. "I know it was scary, but Will's going to be well looked after. A broken leg mends quickly, and Will's healthy and strong. He was awake and talking to us, that's the important thing."

Chloe nodded. She supposed her grandad was right, but Will's leg had been all twisted and wrong-looking.

At last the phone rang, and Chloe spilled her drink all over the table.

Grandad reached for the phone before Chloe could grab it. "Hello, love. What's happening?"

Chloe hovered next to Grandad trying to hear, but it was mostly just *Mm-hm* and *Right*, from his end. She couldn't hear Mum properly.

Finally Grandad put down the phone.

"Didn't she want to talk to me?" Chloe asked, sounding rather hurt.

"She didn't have long, Chlo. Will's going to have an operation on his leg. She needed to be with him."

Chloe gaped at him. "An operation? But I thought he'd just have plaster put on it? Isn't that what you do for broken legs? That's what Maddy had when she broke her arm."

Grandad nodded. "It's quite a bad break – he fell a long way. He's going to have some special pins put in it, to hold together the bone while it mends. Don't worry, they do it all the time."

"Is Will going to have to stay in hospital for long?" Chloe asked, tracing patterns in hot chocolate on the plastic tablecloth. She'd wiped it up, but not very well.

Jess came and stood with her paws on Grandad's knee. She could hear them talking about Will. Where was he? When was he coming home?

"For a while," Grandad replied. "Mum wasn't sure. I'm going to stay here for a couple of nights to look after you."

Chloe felt her throat tighten. She had thought Will would be home tonight. Staying in hospital sounded scary.

Jess looked at Chloe. Was she worried about Will? What was going on? She whimpered, staring up at Chloe and Grandad hopefully. But Chloe just turned away and walked quickly out of the room, her eyes filling with tears.

"Let's leave her to calm down," Grandad murmured to Jess.

Jess stared up at him with big, sad eyes. Everyone was upset, and the house felt strange without Will. She wanted him to come home and play fetch with her in the garden.

Grandad sighed and tickled her

behind the ears. "I know, Jess. I want him home too. But it's just going to be us for a while."

The last week of the summer term was usually brilliant fun. But this year, everything seemed different. Will and Chloe normally walked to school together, because it was only just round the corner, and Will was in Year 6 and old enough to be sensible, Mum said. But all that week, Chloe had to walk to school with Grandad, because she couldn't go by herself. Jess came too, as Grandad said she really needed some exercise.

Chloe missed Will, and Mum and Dad too. They were spending a lot of time at the hospital with Will, and Grandad was going to stay at Chloe's house for the rest of the week to help. She loved Grandad, but she couldn't help feeling a bit left out. At least she had pony camp to look forward to. She and her friend Maddy were spending the second week of the holidays staying at a riding centre, where they'd each get to look after their own special pony all week. They were going pony-trekking and they'd be learning to jump, too. Chloe couldn't wait.

Maddy met them halfway to school as usual. She knew all about Chloe's problems with Jess, but she adored dogs too.

"She's so lovely," Maddy told Chloe, as Jess trotted alongside them. "I do know what you mean about her being boisterous, but she's so cute!"

Chloe sighed. Even though Maddy was her best friend, and she was trying really hard to understand how Chloe felt about Jess, she just couldn't. Maddy loved dogs almost as much as Will!

On Tuesday after school, Mum picked Chloe up in the car to take her to visit Will. She'd seen him for five minutes the day before, but he'd still been sleepy after the operation, and she wasn't sure he'd really known she was there. Chloe was desperate to see him, but a bit nervous at the same time. She knew he was bound to ask about Jess, and she didn't know what to say.

Chloe was starting to worry about the puppy. She spent most of her time moping in her basket, or perched on the window seat in the living room, where she usually sat to watch for Will walking home from school. Obviously she was waiting for him to come, and whenever she heard Mum or Dad pulling up in the car she would rush to the door barking excitedly, her plumy tail wagging. Then as soon as she realized Will wasn't with them, she would slink sadly back to her basket.

Will had a big cast on his leg, but otherwise he was his old self. Except that he hated having to keep still.

Chloe perched on the edge of Will's bed, while Mum went over to speak to one of the nurses.

"I can't believe I'm going to be stuck in bed for ages!" he groaned.

"Does it hurt?" Chloe asked, biting her lip.

"No, it's all right, I've got medicine to stop it hurting. It's itchy though." Will frowned. "Chloe, how's Jess? Is she missing me? Mum says she's fine, but I think she's just saying anything to make me feel better."

Chloe glanced over at Mum, who was still talking to the nurse. She knew what he meant. But she didn't want to upset Will either. Worrying about Jess would only make him feel worse.

"She's OK," Chloe said carefully. "She does miss you, but Grandad's taking her for walks, and she comes with us to school and back."

"But Grandad can't run, Chloe. He's too old! Jess needs loads of exercise. And I was supposed to take her to dog-training in the holidays." He looked worried. "Couldn't you go for walks with Grandad?" Will pleaded. "I know you're nervous with Jess, but if Grandad was there too…"

Chloe looked at her fingers. "We all walk to school together," she repeated. But she knew that wasn't really what Will meant.

"Come on, Chloe. Will needs to have a rest now. You can come back and see him soon." Mum had finished talking, and was looking at Will's pale face with concern.

Chloe hardly spoke on the way home, until they were just turning into their road. "How long is Will going to be there for?" she asked suddenly.

"I'm really not sure, Chloe," Mum answered. "He ought to have been able to come home soon after the operation, but the nurse said they're a bit worried that the bone pieces haven't fitted back together properly yet. It could be a while – a few weeks, even."

"Weeks?" Chloe whispered in horror. She hadn't thought it could possibly be that long. She would miss his stupid jokes. And Jess would be heartbroken.

The puppy was waiting hopefully by the door when they got in, and her drooping ears made Chloe feel so guilty. She'd said to Will that

Jess was OK, but now she looked so miserable. Chloe sighed. If she'd told Will that, it would have made him miserable too. There was nothing he could do about it, stuck in hospital.

But I could help, Chloe told herself. *I could try and cheer Jess up.*

She followed Jess into the kitchen, and watched as she slumped down into her basket. Chloe felt so sorry for her, sitting there with her head hanging.

"Hey, Jess," she said gently, crouching down by the basket.

Jess ignored her. She wanted Will, and he still hadn't come back to her. She didn't like it when he went to school every day, but at least he always came home. Where was he now? And why hadn't he taken her with him?

Chloe nervously darted out a hand to pat Jess, but she patted her too hard, when Jess wasn't expecting it.

Jess was feeling so upset that when Chloe touched her, she jumped round and barked sharply, showing her teeth. What was going on? She stared angrily at Chloe, who was scrambling away, crying. Silly girl!

Why couldn't Chloe just leave her alone?

Chapter Three

Chloe kept away from Jess after that. Her behaviour had brought back all those bad memories of the dog in the park. Chloe visited Will, and spoke to him on the phone a couple of times, but whenever he asked her about Jess, she just said that Grandad was taking her for lots of walks and wriggled out of saying any more.

Grandad really loved dogs, and Jess liked him, but it wasn't the same as racing all over the park with Will. The puppy was bursting with energy, and a couple of short walks a day just weren't enough. Jess was used to a quick walk before school, and then another really long one with Will and Dad later on. But Dad was working late so he could fit in visiting Will in hospital. He didn't have much time for dog-walking. Collies needed so much exercise and Jess really hated being stuck in the house. She was bored.

It was the first morning of the holidays, so Jess hadn't even had her walk to school. She wandered round the house with her lead, looking hopeful, but Mum was busy sorting out some books to take to Will, and Jess knew Chloe wouldn't take her. Mum had encouraged Jess to go out into the garden, but that was no fun without someone to play with. She looked around the kitchen, trying to find something interesting to do. She pushed her squeaky bone across the floor for a while, but what she really needed was Will to throw it for her to chase.

Her bone was up against the kitchen cupboards now, so Jess scrabbled with one paw to get it back into the middle of the floor. But her claws caught on the cupboard door instead. It opened a little way, and then bounced shut.

Jess stared at it, fascinated. Then she carefully hooked her claws round the edge of the door again. Again, the door bounced and banged.

The next time, she pulled it a little too hard, and it didn't bang back. Jess went to nudge the door again with her nose, but then she caught a delicious and interesting whiff from the cupboard.

There was food in there. Jess used her nose to push the door further open and found the cereal packets.

"Oh no! Mu-um!" Chloe was standing in the kitchen doorway, staring at Jess, who looked back rather guiltily. She was surrounded by chewed-up cardboard and an awful lot of cornflakes.

"What's the matter? Oh, Jess!" Mum had come downstairs and was gazing at the mess in horror. "You bad dog," she said crossly. "What a waste. I hope you're not going to be sick now."

Jess flattened herself to the floor and whined miserably, backing towards her basket. She hadn't meant to be bad. The cereal had smelled so good, and the cardboard boxes had been fun to tear up with her teeth...

171

Mum sighed. "Oh, Jess. It isn't really your fault. You need a walk, don't you?"

Jess thumped her tail on the floor, just once, but she kept down, watching Mum clear up the mess. She was sorry, but she still felt grumpy and bored. She desperately wanted something to do.

Chloe helped her mum with the tidying up. When they'd finished, Mum gave her a hug. "Not the best way to spend the first day of the holidays, is it? Shall we go out for an ice cream together after we've been to see Will this afternoon? I feel like I've hardly seen you recently."

Chloe hugged her back, nearly spilling a dustpan full of cornflakes. "Yes, please! Thanks, Mum!" She danced over to empty the cornflakes in the bin. "Don't worry about having to go to the hospital so much. I'll be at pony camp next week with Maddy, so you won't need to worry about me then."

She turned round smiling, but then her eyes widened as she saw her mother's face. "What is it?"

"Oh, Chloe! I never called them! It was one of my jobs for the day after Will had his accident, and I never phoned them up to book!" Mum looked horrified. "Where's the brochure? I'll ring them now."

She grabbed the phone, and Chloe watched her making the call. Her mum frowned a little as she explained, and then looked terribly disappointed and guilty. Chloe knew what Mum was going to say before she even put down the phone.

"I'm so sorry. They're all booked up. They've promised to call me if there's a cancellation, but they didn't sound very hopeful. Oh, Chlo, I feel dreadful…"

Chloe stared down at the ground. She wanted to say it was OK, she knew Mum had had other things on her mind. But she had been looking forward to this for so long! She and Maddy had spent ages at school talking about it, and drawing pictures of the ponies they might get to look after. How was she going to tell Maddy? It would ruin her holiday too!

She swallowed hard, trying not to yell at Mum. She knew she hadn't done it on purpose. But it was so unfair!

She dashed out of the kitchen, scrambled up the stairs to her room and flung herself on to her bed, crying. Mum spent all this time worrying about Will, and she'd just forgotten about her. She mattered too, didn't she?

She cried so much that her head ached, and then she actually fell asleep, in the middle of the day.

Mum came in just after she'd woken up, which made Chloe think she'd probably been hanging around outside her room, for a while. She had a plate with a sandwich and some biscuits on it.

"You missed lunch," she said gently. "Cheese and ketchup, look." It was Chloe's favourite. She wiped her eyes and took the plate gratefully.

"I spoke to Maddy's mum and explained. I said I'd arrange something really special for you girls later in the holidays."

Chloe just nodded.

"I really am sorry, Chlo."

She looked sorry, and Chloe leaned against her shoulder. Crying made her feel awful, and she felt guilty now as well. At least she wasn't stuck in hospital like Will. "I know," she muttered.

"Are you still going to come with me to visit Will tonight?" Mum asked. "I know he's looking forward to seeing you. He asked if you could bring him some DS games."

Chloe nodded. "Mmm. I know which ones he likes. I'll find them when I've eaten this."

"Thanks, Chlo. You're a star." Mum kissed the top of her head, and went back downstairs.

Chloe didn't feel like a star. She felt lonely and miserable. She ate the biscuits, but she didn't really enjoy them, and then she got up to go and fetch Will's games from his bedroom.

She was searching through the pile on his shelf, when a tiny noise made her turn round sharply.

She hadn't noticed that Jess was lying on Will's bed, staring at her, her eyes looking even darker than usual and so sad. For once, Chloe didn't feel that horrible jump of fright that she got when a dog was too close. Jess just seemed so unhappy.

"You look like I feel…" Chloe joked, but it wasn't really funny. "Mum isn't cross with you any more, Jess, honestly."

Jess gazed at Chloe, and thought she looked sad too. She whined, and Chloe nodded.

"I know. You miss Will, don't you?" Chloe picked up the games, then wriggled herself over to lean against Will's bed. "Me too, Jess."

Jess gave a huge sigh, and Chloe giggled. "That was right in my ear." She looked at Jess, whose nose was hanging over the edge of the bed right next to her, and very gently stroked her.

Jess closed her eyes and sighed again, gratefully, as Chloe scratched behind her ears. It felt so nice to have somebody fuss over her.

Chloe lay in bed that night feeling too hot to sleep. Mum had said she thought it might thunder, but even though a storm would probably cool everything down, Chloe hoped she was wrong. She hated thunderstorms. She turned over and yawned. She was tired, but she was never going to be able to sleep in this sticky room…

She was woken hours later by a huge crash of thunder. Her room was still lit up by lightning, which meant the storm was right overhead. Chloe sat up, clutching the duvet around her shoulders. Another flash! The horrible blue-white light sent everything into scary shadows, and she shivered, waiting for the thunder.

Suddenly a little black-and-white body hurtled through her bedroom door, making Chloe squeak with surprise. Jess flung herself on to Chloe's bed, whimpering in fear.

"Oh, Jess, are you scared of thunder too?" Chloe cuddled the puppy close, forgetting to be frightened, either of Jess or the thunder. As the next thunderclap cracked overhead, Jess cowered against her, letting Chloe wrap her arms around her small black ears to shut out the noise. "Ssshh, ssshh, it's OK. It'll go away soon."

Jess licked her hand gratefully. She couldn't have stayed in the kitchen, not with those crashing noises and that awful prickly feel in the air. She really wanted Will, but Chloe would do. It was nice to be cuddled, and she was making good sounds, shushing noises that made the crashing seem not so bad.

She could feel Chloe's heart thudding so quickly. She was scared too, Jess thought. She licked her again, and then snuggled closer as another growl of thunder rumbled round the house.

Chloe lay there, jumping every so often as the thunder rang out, but mostly thinking over and over, *I'm cuddling Jess. I'm holding a dog! I'd never have thought that she'd be scared of thunder, when she's so bouncy and loud.* "You're even worse than me, Jess." She giggled, and Jess licked her under the chin.

The thunder was dying away now, to just a few grumbles, and Chloe lay back down, with Jess still cuddled up next to her. "Are you staying, Jess?" she asked.

But Jess was asleep already, curled in a little ball in the crook of Chloe's arm.

Chapter Four

Jess was still there when Chloe woke up the next morning, snuggled down the side of her bed. Chloe smiled delightedly – it was just like she'd imagined having a dog would be. Jess yawned, showing a huge length of pink tongue, and rolled over on to her back, still fast asleep. She lay there with her paws folded on her chest, snoring a little, until Chloe woke her up by giggling too much.

"Sorry, Jess. You looked so funny."

Jess let out another enormous yawn, then gave Chloe a big face-washing lick.

"Urgh. Now I'm really awake." Chloe got out of bed and followed Jess downstairs to the kitchen, where Mum was making toast.

"I was wondering where Jess had got to!" Mum said, looking slightly surprised. "You slept late! I was just about to come and wake you up. It's holiday club this morning, remember?"

Chloe nodded. Her mum worked part-time at the library, and so in the mornings she and Will usually went to a holiday club at one of the other schools nearby. Even though she didn't normally hang around with Will – he stuck with the boys, mostly – it would feel weird being there without him.

Jess watched sadly through the front window as they got into the car without her. She'd been hoping for a walk. She had that itchy, bored feeling again. She trotted back into the kitchen and out into the garden through her dog-door. She sniffed around for a while and snapped at a few butterflies, then she just lay on her side in a sunny patch, flicking her tail idly.

A beetle wandered past her nose, and Jess rolled over to stare at it as it trundled off between her paws. She crept after it, tail wagging slightly, and watched it climb under some stones in the flower bed. Where had it gone?

Jess pawed at the stones, but the beetle had gone. She scrabbled some more, then dug furiously, her paws spraying up stones and earth. The beetle was long gone, but the digging was fun. Jess happily clawed and scraped and scratched, loving the exercise.

Then she fell asleep, her nose in a pile of earth, worn out and snoozing blissfully.

"Jess!"

Jess sat up with a jump, blinking sleepily, and saw that Chloe was there, looking down at her with her hands to her mouth.

"Oh, Jess, Mum's going to go mad. Dad gave her that plant for her birthday." Chloe quickly fetched a trowel from the garden shed to scoop some of the earth back into the flower bed. "We have to tidy up. Maybe she won't notice."

But it was too late. Chloe's mum was standing by the back door, looking horrified. In fact, she looked more than horrified, she looked furious.

"You bad dog! Look at this mess! Oh, I don't believe it! My beautiful camellia..." She crouched down to look at the plants that Jess had rooted up.

Jess hung her head sadly. She'd only been playing...

"I think she was bored, Mum," Chloe said quickly. "Don't be cross with her, please. She misses Will, and all the walks he and Dad used to take her on. And now Grandad's not staying any more, she's hardly getting any exercise at all."

Chloe stroked Jess, feeling her shiver. It was obvious she hated being shouted at. Chloe frowned. "Mum, could me and Maddy take Jess for a walk? Just to the park. We could run around with her and work off some of her energy; I'm sure she wouldn't be so naughty then."

Mum shook her head. "You're not old enough, Chlo. And I thought you were terrified of dogs! And Jess is such a handful. But you're right, she does need more exercise."

Chloe helped her try to fill in the earth around the camellia again. "Mum, you let Will walk me to school all last year, and he's only a year older than me. And I'll be with Maddy, too! She'll help me with Jess. We'll be fine!"

Her mum sighed. "Well, it might be worth a try. I'm sure she's only being naughty because we're not spending enough time with her."

Chloe threw her arms around Mum. "Excellent! I'll go and ring Maddy!"

"This is great, Chloe. I can't believe you aren't nervous of Jess any more." Maddy was looking admiringly at Chloe walking with Jess on her lead.

Chloe smiled. "I can't either. But it's brilliant."

Jess was scampering along happily, sniffing the interesting smells and hoping they were going to the park so she could run really fast, like she did with Will. She still wished he would come back, but Chloe was her person now, too. Chloe had looked after her during that horrible, frightening night, and that made her special.

They raced all over the park for a whole hour, until the girls were exhausted, although Jess was still bright and bouncy.

"She's not tired at all!" Maddy panted, collapsing on to a bench. "Look at her, she wants to dash off again!"

Jess barked excitedly. She could see a

squirrel scurrying along between those trees, and she loved chasing squirrels. She looked up hopefully at Chloe and tugged on the lead.

"Sorry, Jess, we've got to get home. I promised Mum we'd be back by five." Chloe turned to walk Jess out of the park, and Jess gave the squirrel a last longing look and followed her.

But then the squirrel changed direction and started to run along the grass almost in front of Jess's nose. It was too much to bear. She gave an enormous bark and flung herself after the squirrel.

Chloe gasped as she felt the lead almost pulling out of her hand. "Hey! Jess, no. Come back!"

Jess was so strong. Chloe tried

desperately to get her under control, but she was only just managing to hold on as Jess dragged her after the squirrel. They galloped over the grass, and then Jess cut across one of the tarmac paths that ran through the park. Chloe tripped on the edge of the grass and went flying, finally letting go of her lead.

Jess sped up. She was going to catch a squirrel at last! But the squirrel had made it to the trees, and all Jess could do was bark crossly at it as it disappeared into the leafy branches. Disappointed, she turned to go back to Chloe.

Chloe! There she was, lying on the path. She was crying! Jess let out a terrified whimper and raced over, throwing herself on to the ground next to Chloe and whining miserably.

Chloe had scraped her knee on the tarmac, and blood was dripping down her leg. Maddy was trying to wipe it up with a tissue, but it was a nasty cut.

"Oh, Jess, it's OK." Chloe sniffed. "Don't be upset." She could see why Jess was frightened, and she felt so sorry for her. Will had been hurt, and he'd gone away. Now Jess thought that she was going to go away too.

"Are you all right to walk?" Maddy asked, helping Chloe to her feet.

"I'm fine," Chloe said. "Let's go home."

Maddy took Jess by the lead. "Just don't go too fast, Jess, OK?"

They slowly made their way back, with Chloe leaning on Maddy and Jess trotting obediently alongside her.

Chloe's mum was watching out for them through the front window. She looked worried.

"Are we really late?" Chloe muttered.

Maddy frowned. "A bit. And she wasn't sure about letting us go, was she?"

Mum flung open the front door. "Chloe, you promised me five — Oh no, what have you done?" She helped Chloe inside, and Jess and Maddy crept in behind them, not wanting to be noticed.

"What happened?" Mum asked, getting down the first-aid box. She looked very upset – much more upset than she ought to be about just a scraped knee, Chloe thought.

"Jess ran after a squirrel and I tripped," she explained, trying not to make it sound too serious.

"That dog again!" Mum said crossly.

"She didn't mean to hurt me! She was really sorry – she was whimpering," Chloe protested. But she could see Mum wasn't really listening.

"She's too wilful. I don't know what we're going to do with her," Mum said, dabbing at Chloe's knee with a wipe.

"Oh, she isn't really, Mum!" Chloe protested, giving Maddy a horrified look. "She's lovely! She didn't mean to hurt me."

Jess sat in her basket, her eyes swivelling between Mum and Chloe, shivering at the loud, upset voices. Mum kept looking at her as though this was all her fault. And Jess had a horrible feeling that it was.

Chapter Five

Will smiled and shook his head as he spotted Chloe walking up the children's ward, a big plaster on her knee. "I know you miss me, Chlo, but cutting your leg off so you can stay in hospital too, that's just dim... Seriously, what did you do?"

Chloe grinned at him. "I took Jess for a walk! Well, me and Maddy did."

She looked down at the plaster and shrugged. "But Jess wanted to chase a squirrel, and I tripped…"

Will beamed. "That's brilliant!"

"Hey!"

"Not your knee! Brilliant that you took Jess out. Thanks, Chlo. I'd been really worrying about her."

Chloe sighed and glanced over at her mum, who was talking to the doctor. "I'm not sure Mum's going to let me take her out again, though," she whispered. "She was so cross. Jess has been really naughty in the last couple of days."

Will thought for a moment. "Well, if you really can't talk Mum round, perhaps you can wear off some of her energy in the garden. She loves playing fetch, and you could try hiding one of her toys and getting her to play hide-and-seek, that's fun. Then maybe she'll be a bit less mad."

Chloe nodded. "Good idea. Anyway, I might still get Mum to give in."

"You just need to stretch your legs, don't you, Jessie?" Chloe murmured, stroking Jess's silky black-and-white back, as they leaned against the sofa watching TV.

Jess let out a huge sigh, as if in agreement, then slumped down with her head in Chloe's lap.

Chloe had spent ages persuading her mum that Jess had only tripped her up by accident. But Mum was still saying that she didn't think it was a good idea for Chloe and Maddy to take Jess out again. Chloe was also worried about what her mum had said about not knowing what to do with Jess. What did that mean? She was scared that her mum might want to send Jess back to the breeder they'd got her from. Will would be heartbroken.

And it wasn't just Will. Chloe would miss Jess so much, too, she realized now. She was determined to turn Jess into the most perfect dog ever, so Mum wouldn't want to get rid of her. But that meant they had to go out for more walks. Chloe was sure that Jess was only playing up because she needed loads more exercise, and the occasional short walks she was getting with Grandad just weren't enough. She'd spent the morning playing in the garden with Jess, like Will had suggested, but she was sure that Jess really wanted more space for a good long run.

Eventually, after a whole day of begging, Mum agreed to let Chloe and Maddy take Jess out. But she made Chloe take her mobile phone, so they could call home if anything went wrong.

Luckily, Jess seemed to know that she had to be on her best behaviour. She walked sedately all the way to the park, trotting along next to Chloe. Chloe and Maddy smiled at each other as a couple of old ladies commented on what a well-behaved dog she was.

"I wish we could get them to go and say that to my mum!" Chloe whispered, and Maddy giggled.

Chloe's leg was still a bit too sore for her to run really fast, so Maddy took Jess's lead when they got to the park.

Jess looked up at Maddy and Chloe, her ears pricked, but she didn't race off.

"What's up, Jess?" Maddy asked her gently.

Chloe leaned down to stroke her, and Jess nuzzled her gently, pressing her cool, damp nose into Chloe's hand. She rubbed Jess's ears. "It's OK, Jess. You go! Run with Maddy!"

"But not too fast!" Maddy added, smiling.

Jess wagged her tail delightedly, swishing it like a flag, and sprinted away, but she kept coming back to check on Chloe, who was sitting on one of the benches.

"She's really worried about you," Maddy said, panting. Jess had just raced to the other side of the trees and back. "She's such a sweetheart."

Jess sat on the path, laid her muzzle on Chloe's lap and stared up at her anxiously. Was Chloe all right? She swept her tail back and forth across the path when Chloe beamed at her.

Maddy flopped on to the bench too. "We should head back, shouldn't we?" she asked, checking her watch.

Chloe nodded. "Let's go home past the shops to give Jess a change," she suggested. She took the lead from Maddy and got to her feet.

Jess looked up at them both, and her tail stopped wagging. Home? Already? But she wanted to run some more! That had hardly felt like a walk at all.

"Do you think your mum will let you take Jess out on your own next week, when I'm at pony camp?" Maddy asked, as they walked through the park gates.

Chloe frowned. She hadn't really thought about that. "I haven't mentioned it yet, but I can't see her saying yes. She'd be too worried something might happen to us. Maybe I can ask Grandad to come with me…"

"Do you mind if I nip in and buy a magazine?" Maddy asked, as they went past the corner shop.

Chloe shook her head. "Course not. We'll wait for you outside. Sit, Jess!"

Jess looked at Chloe doubtfully, and Chloe gently pushed her to sit down. She'd been reading up on the internet about dog-training, and she'd tried practising with Jess in the garden, but they weren't very good at it yet. Eventually Jess sat, and Chloe fussed over her lovingly.

Maddy took ages. Chloe could see her through the window, dithering about which magazine to buy.

She gazed down at her feet, thinking sadly about pony camp and how cool it would have been. But then, if she'd gone Jess would have been really lonely without her, she supposed. Maybe it was all for the best.

Jess soon got bored of sitting still and watching people going in and out of the shop. Lots of them had interesting things in their bags, though. She sniffed hopefully. Delicious-smelling things.

Suddenly, Jess pulled sharply at her

lead, and Chloe gasped as she dragged
it out of her hand. Before Chloe could
catch her, Jess was right outside the
shop door, rooting in a big shopping
bag which a lady had put down while
she found her car keys.

"Jess, no!" Chloe squeaked, horrified, as the lady tried to pull her bag away.

"Is this your dog?" she demanded furiously. "What on earth were you doing, letting go of her like that?"

"I'm really sorry!" Chloe said, blushing scarlet. "Oh, Jess…" She finally managed to grab Jess's lead and pull her out of the shopping bag, but it was too late. She had a biscuit in her mouth, and there was a packet sticking out of the bag, ripped open by her sharp little teeth.

"She's eating my biscuits!" the lady shouted. Chloe thought she might explode, she looked so cross.

"I'm so sorry, I'll pay for them," she gasped, frantically digging in her skirt pocket for her purse, while trying to hold on to Jess's collar with her other hand.

Jess had finished the delicious biscuit, but she was beginning to realize that she'd done something wrong. The lady with the bag was shouting at Chloe. Jess squirmed behind Chloe's legs to hide.

Chloe quickly pressed a pound coin into the lady's hand, muttering, "Sorry!" again. As she pulled Jess away, she could hear the lady behind her, telling everyone coming out of the shop that little girls shouldn't be allowed to walk dogs they couldn't control.

"What happened?" said Maddy, as she came out of the shop, clutching her magazine.

"Jess stole that lady's biscuits!"

Chloe whispered to her friend. "It was so embarrassing! I don't think I'll ever dare go in that shop again!"

When they got home, Chloe carefully avoided telling Mum about their walk – except that Jess had been good in the park. She went out into the garden and lay on the rug under the apple tree in the shade. It was so hot.

Jess lay down next to her, panting and wagging her tail as the bees buzzed past her nose.

Chloe reached out to stroke her. "What am I going to do with you, Jess?" she muttered. "Only two walks. One cut knee for me, one stolen biscuit for you. This isn't working out very well, is it?"

Chapter Six

Grandad came over the next day to look after Chloe while Mum and Dad went to the hospital, and as soon as they'd shut the front door behind them, Chloe pulled him over to the kitchen table to sit down and talk.

"What's the matter, Chlo?" Grandad grinned at her. "You're looking very serious."

Chloe huffed out a sigh. "It is serious! I've tried everything, but Jess can't stop getting into trouble. Mum's really cross with her and I'm worried she might take her back to the dog breeder."

Grandad looked down at Jess, who was fighting with her stretchy rubber bone under the table. "I'm sure your mum wouldn't do that. She hasn't said anything to me. What's Jess been doing?"

Chloe explained about the cereal, and the plants, and her knee, and then the stolen biscuits. It did sound rather awful when it was all in a long list, she realized.

Grandad nodded slowly. "I didn't know she was so upset with Jess, but I can see why… It's been really hard for her and your dad, you know, worrying so much about Will. And they're worried about you too, Chlo. Your mum thinks it's really spoiling your holiday."

"If I could get Jess to behave well and go for walks without being afraid of what she might do, I'd be having a brilliant summer," Chloe replied.

"But you're already making a big difference," Grandad pointed out, reaching across the table to cover her hand with his. "Think back to the day of Will's accident – just think about how you were with Jess. I felt so sad, watching you. It looked like you secretly wanted to play with Jess and Will, but you couldn't make yourself. And now look at you! I know the walks didn't turn out too well, but at least you went! And you haven't given up on Jess, even after she's got you into trouble. I'm so proud of you."

Chloe went pink and looked down at the table, feeling embarrassed. Dad had spotted her cuddling Jess the day before and told her it was great that she seemed to be getting on so well with the puppy, but no one had said it as nicely as that before.

"But it isn't making her any better behaved, Grandad. I just don't know what to try next."

Grandad hugged her. "Honestly, your mum won't send her back. But we don't want her getting any more stressed out than she is already." He nodded thoughtfully. "What that dog needs is a training class."

"Oh yes!" Chloe bounced in her chair. "Will was going to take her, but it clashed with football. He was planning to do it in the holidays instead, but then we all forgot about it after the accident."

"How about it then? You, me and Jess. Let's find ourselves a trainer. Come on, Chlo, show me some of those computer skills. Let's go and see what's on round here."

Ten minutes later, Chloe and Grandad had found a training class that was being run in the church hall round the corner. "Look, there's a class starting this Tuesday," Grandad pointed out. "Perfect. Something fun for us to do while Maddy's away, stop you feeling too sad about that pony club thingummy."

"Pony camp." Chloe giggled. "Can we call now, Grandad? I hope they aren't full up."

Luckily, they weren't. Grandad put down the phone, looking very pleased with himself.

"We can go?" Chloe asked eagerly. She was standing next to him, with Jess waltzing excitedly round her legs. Jess could tell that something good was happening. Chloe sounded so happy.

Grandad nodded. "And when I told Mike, the trainer, that Jess was a Border collie, he mentioned that he does agility sessions too. So I've signed us up for a taster in a few weeks' time."

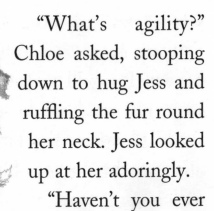

"What's agility?" Chloe asked, stooping down to hug Jess and ruffling the fur round her neck. Jess looked up at her adoringly.

"Haven't you ever seen it on TV?" Grandad replied. "It's a bit like show-jumping, but for dogs. Jess isn't old enough for real agility classes yet, but he thought she'd enjoy the taster session."

Chloe beamed. "Jess would love that."

"I'm sure she would. Mike said it's great for collies; it works off loads of their energy. I thought it sounded like just what we need!"

218

Chloe was rather nervous about the first training session. What if Jess didn't behave? It would be really embarrassing if she just wouldn't do as she was told. And Chloe was a tiny bit worried about all those other dogs too. She wasn't scared of Jess any more, but she wasn't sure how she'd feel about a hall full of dogs.

Luckily, there were only five in their class, and they were all puppies too. Two Labradors, one black and one chocolate, a cocker spaniel, and one breed that Chloe didn't recognize. His owner said he was a mixed bag.

Jess adored the class. Everyone fussed over her and said how beautiful she was, and Chloe spent ages telling her she was a good dog, every time she did as she was told.

"She's doing really well." Mike, the trainer, crouched down by Jess and patted her gently. "Let's see you walk up the hall, turn at the end and come back. Don't pull her, and walk slowly, OK? Lots of praise."

Chloe looked down at Jess lovingly – "Come on, Jess, walk," she said, keeping her voice gentle but firm, like she'd been told.

Jess showed off happily, trotting along right next to Chloe and turning perfectly, without Chloe having to pull her.

"Great. Give her one of your treats, Chloe. She's a natural." Mike looked really pleased.

"You are such a clever girl, Jess!" Chloe said, holding out a dog biscuit.

Jess gulped down the delicious meaty biscuit, wagging her tail happily. She loved dog training!

At the end of the class, Grandad walked over. He'd been watching from the back of the hall, and Chloe had asked him to take some photos to show Will when she went to visit.

"We were so lucky there was a course starting this week. Jess seemed to really enjoy herself." Grandad smiled. "I'm sure she'll love that agility taster session, too."

On their way home, Jess walked close to Chloe, feeling happily tired after the class. She wanted to go home and curl up in her basket, then later maybe Chloe would play those fun games with her in the garden.

There might even be more of the yummy treats.

Chloe's mum was delighted that it had gone so well. "I'm going to have to come and watch one of these classes," she suggested. "It sounds as though you and Jess are doing brilliantly."

"We've got beginners' training on Tuesdays and Thursdays for the next four weeks," Chloe explained.

"Are you coming with me to see Will?" Mum asked.

Chloe nodded excitedly. "Yes, I want to tell him how fantastic Jess was at the class. He's going to be so proud of her! I didn't tell him we were going, in case Jess behaved really badly."

Will was watching a DVD on the screen above his bed, but he turned it off as soon as he saw Mum and Chloe. "Wow, it's good to see you," he said, grinning. "Mum, have they said how much longer I have to be in for?"

Mum shook her head. "I'm supposed to talk to Dr Bedford today. Hopefully not much longer, now you've started physiotherapy."

Will made a face. "It's good being allowed to move, but I'm so slow! It's going to be ages before I can go for runs in the park with Jess. How is she?"

Chloe beamed at him and pulled out her camera to show him the photos Grandad had taken. "She's brilliant! Look!"

Will stared at them, frowning. "You

took her to dog training? But I was going to do that!"

Chloe looked at him in surprise. She had thought he'd be pleased. "I know, but—"

"I was really looking forward to it!" Will said angrily. "She's my dog!"

"Actually, Will, she's a family dog," Mum said gently. "I know you've spent the most time with her, but Chloe's been looking after her really well. You'll be able to go to the classes too when you're better."

But Will was still scowling, and he hardly spoke to Chloe for the rest of the visit.

Chapter Seven

When Jess sneaked into Chloe's room that night, she could feel that something wasn't right. Ever since Chloe had come home, she'd been so quiet. She'd petted Jess and played with her, but she hadn't been quite the same.

Jess stood by Chloe's bed and looked up hopefully.

"Hello, Jess!" Chloe smiled and patted the duvet. "Come on! Up!"

Jess bounced on to the bed and settled herself on Chloe's tummy, staring into her face. "Oof, you're heavy," Chloe said. "It's nice though. You're like the best sort of teddy bear." She sighed.

Jess put her head to one side and whined questioningly. What was wrong?

"I know you don't really understand, but you're a very good listener," Chloe murmured, tickling her under the chin.

Jess wagged her tail sleepily and closed her eyes. She was still listening, but she was worn out after all that hard work at the class.

"I hadn't really thought about it until we went to the hospital this evening," Chloe said, gazing at the ceiling.

"Of course I'm still looking forward to Will coming home, but it's going to be hard when he comes back, too."

Jess flicked one ear thoughtfully as Chloe mentioned Will.

"I know Mum said you're a family dog, but really you've always been mostly his. You're not going to want to play with me, once you've got Will back..."

Chloe sighed and looked down at Jess again. "I'm not even sure we can keep going to dog training, Will was so upset..." Then she smiled, sadly. Jess was fast asleep, floppy as a rag doll, stretched out on her tummy.

"I'll make the most of you while I can," she whispered, stroking Jess lovingly.

Grandad was very firm with Chloe when she suggested giving up the dog-training classes until Will could take Jess instead.

"No. Absolutely not, Chlo. That's not fair on you or Jess. You saw how much she loved training, and she needs it too. She was getting into bad habits. It's sad for Will, but he loves Jess, and he'll understand. There'll be plenty more classes that he can take her to. I'm going to see him this afternoon, so I'll have a chat with him."

Chloe hugged him with relief. She really didn't want to give up the classes – that first one had been so much fun.

When she next went to see Will, he

glared at her as she came up to his bed, and she wondered if he was still cross.

"Grandad says I have to say sorry," Will muttered grumpily. "He says I should be grateful to you for looking after Jess so well." He sighed. "And I am. It's only that I was really looking forward to the classes. But Jess needs training now. I know it's not fair to make her wait."

Chloe beamed at him. "You'll be out of here soon, then you can take her. She's really good," she added.

It was true. They'd had quite a few classes now, as they were twice a week, and Jess was a star at every one. There was going to be a competition at the final training session, Mike had said, and Chloe really wanted Jess to do well.

They'd been practising loads in the garden. She didn't mention training to Will again though; it didn't seem very fair.

She just wished Will could have come to the special agility taster session, too. As she and Grandad watched Mike setting up the course, she knew he would have loved it.

Mike had brought his two adult Border collies to show everybody else what to do. "Aren't they beautiful?" Chloe whispered to Jess. "You're going to look like that, when you're bigger."

Jess wasn't really listening. She was staring eagerly at Mike as he took one of the collies, Marlo, to the start of the course. It had been set up in a big field on a nearby farm.

Jess's tail was twitching with excitement and her eyes sparkled as she watched Marlo set off, speeding round the course, leaping over the jumps, darting in and out of the weaving poles, and shooting through a long pop-up tunnel. He even jumped through a hoop, and then finished by running up a see-saw and tipping it down. Everyone clapped when he and Mike completed the course, and Marlo just shook his ears proudly, as if to say it was nothing.

Mike and another instructor then began to demonstrate how to use the different equipment. Chloe and Jess started with low jumps. Even though Jess was tiny compared to some of the other dogs, she flew over the jumps easily.

Mike watched her, laughing. "Chloe, promise me, when Jess is a year old and can go to proper agility classes, you'll bring her along."

"Oh, does she have to be a year?" Chloe asked disappointedly.

Mike nodded. "Some of the agility equipment isn't suitable for pups because they're still growing. Things like the weaving poles – those sticks Marlo was going in and out of – they can hurt a young dog's back."

Chloe nodded. "I think she'd love to go to a proper class, once she's old enough."

"Agility is great for collies; they're so bright and so energetic. And it uses up all that energy too. They can be a real handful when they're bored."

Chloe nodded. "Jess was being so naughty before we came to training," she agreed. "She was a nightmare."

"You should definitely bring her to agility. Did you know some agility teachers run ABC classes?" Mike asked her, grinning. "Anything But Collies. Because they're so good at it, they leave all the other dogs standing!"

When they got back Mum dashed out to meet them and hugged Chloe delightedly. "Will's coming home! Tomorrow! Isn't that wonderful?"

Chloe hugged her back. She had missed Will so much. Although it did hurt a little bit to see Jess jumping up and down, wagging her whole back end, not just her tail, she was so excited. "You're going to be so glad to see him, aren't you?" Chloe said, giving her a stroke. "Will's hardly going to recognize you, your fur's so long now!"

After dinner, she spread herself out on the living-room floor and taped together six big sheets of drawing paper.

"There you are! What are you doing?" Dad asked, peering round the living room door.

"Making a 'Welcome Home' banner for Will. I thought I'd put it in the hallway. Can I tie it on to the banisters?"

"Course you can. That's a really nice idea, Chlo. Do you need any help?"

Chloe shook her head. "Only with the tying. Thanks, Dad."

The banner took ages, outlining the letters, then painting them in with lots of different colours. When she'd finished filling in 'Welcome Home!', Chloe decided to have a break and go and get some juice while it dried.

She came back with her drink and stood at the door to admire her work – which was now decorated with a pattern of blue and red paw prints.

"Jess!" Chloe said crossly. "You walked on it!"

Jess looked up at her guiltily, and gave her tail an apologetic wag. Chloe laughed. "Actually, I bet Will would like it better like this anyway." She smiled to herself, imagining how furious she would have been if Jess had done something like that a few weeks ago. "You just want to welcome him back too, don't you? We'd better wash your paws though, before you track paint everywhere."

Jess and Chloe sat on the window seat, staring out at the road, waiting for Will to come. Jess kept jumping down, running over to the front door, and then dashing back again. She was so excited her tail couldn't stop wagging. Will! Chloe had said Will was coming home!

Chloe peered out of the window. "Yes! There's the car, Jess. They're here!"

Jess shot out into the hallway, barking excitedly and scrabbling at the door.

Chloe opened it, and they stood watching as Will struggled out of the car on his crutches.

Jess looked up at Chloe uncertainly as she saw Will hobbling towards them, but Chloe smiled and shooed her forward. Will was beaming, and calling to  her, so she went to sniff him, and then licked his hands lovingly. She could tell that she shouldn't jump up.

"Good girl, Jess," Mum said gratefully. "I was worried she might be a bit rough."

Will loved the banner. "Great painting, Jess." He chuckled, balancing on one crutch to ruffle her fur. He looked up at Chloe. "Thanks for looking after her. She looks great."

Chloe smiled proudly, but he was saying it as if she didn't have to worry any more. It felt like Will was taking Jess back now. She lagged behind as they went into the house. Feeling as though she ought to let Will and Jess be on their own, she lingered in the hallway. She missed Jess already!

Jess led Will into the living room, and lay down determinedly on his lap as soon as he sat down on the sofa.

"She's not letting you go again," Dad said, laughing.

Jess sighed happily. But then she looked round for Chloe. Why wasn't she here too?

Jess sat up and licked Will's hand, then headed out into the hallway, where Chloe was sitting on the stairs. Jess looked up at her and gave a worried little whine. Why was Chloe all on her own? She took the hem of Chloe's dress in her teeth and tugged, very gently.

Chloe smiled at her, her eyes widening with hope. "You want me to come too?" she whispered, and Jess wagged her tail. Chloe leaned forwards and kissed the top of her head. "You belong to both of us, now, don't you?" she whispered gratefully.

Chapter Eight

"Jess! Jess!" Chloe ran down the stairs, a worried edge creeping into her voice. She couldn't find Jess anywhere. Or Will. But she had a horrible feeling that she knew where they were.

Will had hated being stuck in the house over the last few days. Almost more than he'd hated the hospital. He couldn't ride his bike or skateboard, and even if he wanted to go upstairs Mum or Dad had to help. But not being able to walk Jess was the worst thing of all. He was desperate to take her out. Mum had driven him and Chloe to the park the day after they came back, so that he could watch Jess running around. But poor Jess hadn't understood, and she'd kept coming back to Will and staring at him hopefully, wanting him to join in.

Ever since then, Will had been aching to take Jess out to the park by himself.

"She's really well-behaved now, Mum," he'd pleaded that morning at breakfast. "It isn't far. Now that she's been to dog-training classes, I could take her, no problem."

"Of course you can't!" Mum sounded horrified. "You're only just out of hospital! You need to use your crutches; how can you possibly manage Jess as well?"

But Chloe didn't think Will had been convinced. He'd just scowled into his cereal.

Chloe stopped dead at the bottom of the stairs, her eyes wide. Will's crutches were propped up by the front door, and Jess's lead was gone from its hook.

He'd taken her out, Chloe realized, nibbling her thumbnail anxiously. He'd got so cross with everyone fussing over him that he'd decided to show them, and he'd taken Jess for a walk on his own.

Chloe stared at the door. If she went and told, Mum would have a fit. Better just to go and find them. She reached for the door keys and let herself quietly out of the house.

Jess was walking beautifully, not pulling at all, just like she'd learned at the training classes. But Will was holding her lead strangely, she thought, looking up at him. He kept wobbling. He looked like he wanted to turn back, and they were only halfway to the park. Jess stared up at him and whimpered. Something was wrong.

Will suddenly sat down on someone's front wall, gasping. "Sorry, Jess," he muttered. "I shouldn't have brought you out; it was a stupid idea and now we're stuck."

Jess pulled gently at the lead in his hand, but he tightened his grip. "No, sorry, Jess. We're not going to the park."

Jess whined – she had to make him understand. If he let her go, she could fetch help! She took the lead in her teeth this time and tugged at it harder. Then she walked a couple of steps back in the direction of the house and barked encouragingly at him.

"No, I can't," Will tried to explain. "Oh! *You* want to go home? Do you know the way?" he asked doubtfully.

Home! Jess sat down, wagging her tail. She pulled the lead with her teeth again, and this time he let it go.

"Go home, Jess. Find Chloe," Will told her. The puppy licked his hand reassuringly, before trotting off down the road as fast as she could. She felt anxious – she didn't like running along with her lead trailing like this. But she had to help Will.

Chloe dashed down their street, heading for the park. She really hoped Will hadn't done anything to make his leg worse. What if he'd fallen?

Suddenly she spotted Jess running towards her – on her own. Where was Will?

Jess gave a delighted bark. She'd found Chloe! She jumped up at her, barking again and again, and Chloe hugged her tightly. "Good girl, Jess. Shhh! Where's Will? Can you show me?" she asked, holding Jess's scrabbly front paws.

Jess jumped down immediately and turned back, waiting for Chloe to pick up her lead. Then they raced along the road together.

Will was still sitting on the wall when Jess proudly led Chloe back to him. He was looking very white, and Chloe sat down next to him, wondering if he'd have a go at her if she gave him a hug. She compromised by putting an arm round his shoulder.

"Don't say it," he muttered.

"I didn't!"

Will smiled at her for a second. "Sorry. I should have listened to Mum. It's a good thing Jess was here. She knew what to do – she made me let go of the lead so she could fetch you."

"She's a star," Chloe told him, watching Jess panting contently. "You should come to her training classes, you know. The last beginners' class is on Thursday. It's a special competition lesson. You'd be really proud of her." She stood up and helped him pull himself to his feet. Then they set off slowly down the road.

"Um, maybe," Will said quietly. "I'm sorry I was so jealous before. It's just I was looking forward to taking her."

"You could help me practise with her," Chloe suggested. "Even if the walking bits are difficult, you could do sit and stay. And she needs to learn to behave properly for you too."

"I suppose so." Will looked a bit more cheerful. "Grandad told me about her stealing those biscuits. They ought to have a biscuit-hunt in this competition. Jess would win, wouldn't you?"

Jess barked, ears pricked, and Will burst out laughing.

"I'm never taking her anywhere near a shop ever again." Chloe shuddered. "Come on. If we're quick, Mum might not have noticed we've been gone."

They limped back home, with Jess walking at a snail's pace beside them, giving them both loving looks.

"I can't believe how good she is!" Will told Chloe, as he watched Jess sitting on her own in the middle of the church hall, with a biscuit between her front paws.

"She isn't even looking at it!"

"She knows she'll get it in a minute," Chloe said, but she couldn't keep the proud smile off her face. "All that practice we've done has really helped."

Mike nodded at her, and she walked back to Jess. "Good girl!" she said. "You can eat it now."

Jess gulped down the treat happily. She could see Will grinning at her too.

Mike wrote something on the piece of paper he was holding and looked around the room. "Well done, everyone! That's the end of the competition, so can you all line up along here with your dogs, please, and I'll announce the winners."

Chloe grabbed Will's arm and helped him to the centre of the hall, so that he could line up with Jess, too.

"She's your dog as well," she hissed, as he gave her an *I shouldn't be doing this!* look. "Intermediate training classes start next week, and I've told Mike we're both coming – we can take turns leading her. You can be off your crutches for an hour by then, can't you?"

Will nodded, grinning. "I'm sure I'll manage it."

Mike was walking along the line with a handful of shiny rosettes. "Well, it's been very tight, but we have a winner. Chloe and Will, can you bring Jess out for her first place rosette, please!"

"Jess, you won!" Chloe hugged her, quickly rubbing her cheek against Jess's silky ruff of fur. "Come on, Will!"

As they made their way to the front, Chloe looked round delightedly at Mum and Dad and Grandad, all clapping. Grandad had the camera ready too.

Mike handed Chloe the rosette, and she bent down to pin it to Jess's collar. The puppy looked up at Will on one side and Chloe on the other, both smiling. And she thumped her tail happily on the floor.

Ellie the Homesick Puppy

For Tom, Robin and William

Chapter One

"Megan, you're meant to be packing those books, not reading them!"

Megan looked up guiltily at her mum.

"Sorry! I found this one down the side of my bed, and I'd forgotten I'd even got it. I haven't read it for ages." Megan reluctantly put the book inside a box and sighed.

Mum smiled. "Oh, go on, you can keep it out – we've got a couple more days till we go anyway. You'll go mad without a book to read."

Megan nodded and laid the book on her pillow as Mum headed back downstairs. She sat down on her bed and shook her head disbelievingly.

"A couple more days, Ellie. Only two more nights sleeping in this bedroom," she murmured.

Ellie clambered up on to Megan's knee, wagging her tail, and then licked her hand lovingly. She didn't know why Megan sounded worried, but she wanted to help.

"You're excited too, aren't you?" Megan said, smiling. "You haven't got to go to a new school though, lucky Ellie."

She stroked Ellie's golden ears, and the little puppy shivered with delight. Then she curled up on the duvet again, working herself into a little yellow furry ball.

Moving house was exciting and scary at the same time. Megan's bedroom in the new house was much bigger than this one, which would be great – but then she was really going to miss her best friend Bella, and all her mates from school. They had broken up for the Easter holidays the day before, and everyone in her class had got together to make her a huge card, with all their photos on it and a message from each of them. She'd almost cried when they gave it to her, thinking how they'd all tried so hard to make it special. It was sitting on her desk now, so she could pack it very carefully at the top of one of the boxes, last thing. Megan looked at it and sighed.

It wasn't as if they were actually

moving all that far – only about ten miles; it wasn't the other side of the country, or anything like that. But it meant a new school, of course, and a whole load of new people. *New friends*, Megan told herself firmly.

The best thing was that in two days' time, Megan and Ellie would be able to step out of their back door and ramble wherever they wanted. Here they only had the park, and Megan wasn't allowed to walk Ellie on her own. She knew she was going to have to be very careful going for walks in the countryside near their new house, and every time she mentioned it, Mum kept reminding her about being responsible and not going too far. But all the same, she was practically going to have a wood at the end of her garden! It was going to be brilliant! She'd be able to take Ellie over to her gran's house, too, as Gran lived just about in walking distance from their new house.

Megan gently stroked Ellie's soft golden back, and the little dog gave a sleepy whine and half rolled over, inviting Megan to stroke her tummy. She yawned hugely, showing her very white teeth, and opened her eyes, blinking lovingly up at Megan.

Megan smiled back at her. "I just can't wait to take you for walks in those woods," she whispered happily. "It's going to be the best thing ever!"

Ellie sprang up and gave an excited, hopeful little bark.

Megan laughed. "You heard me say

the W word, didn't you, Ellie-pie? I can't believe you want to go out again, we've only been back home an hour!"

Ellie was wagging her tail madly now, staring up at Megan, but Megan shook her head.

"I'm sorry, Ellie. Mum says I have to pack."

Ellie didn't understand exactly what Megan was saying, but she knew what that tone of voice meant. No walk. She lay back down on the bed, her head resting mournfully on her paws. She knew they'd had a long walk, but now she'd had a little sleep, she felt just like another run.

Megan laughed at her. "You're such an actress, Ellie! You're behaving like I never take you for walks. And it's not fair, because you know I'd love to. But we have to get everything into boxes." She sighed. "And Mum's only given me these ones. She says if I can't get all my stuff in here, I'm going to have to sort some of it out and get rid of it." She looked round her room worriedly. It seemed an awful lot to fit into such a small stack of boxes.

Megan went over to the window sill and started to pack her collection of toy dogs into a box. She had loads, all different breeds, but more than half of them were Labradors, like Ellie. Officially, she was a Yellow Labrador, but Megan thought yellow wasn't the right word at all. Ellie was really a rich honey-golden colour, with pale cream fur on her tummy. Her ears were a shade darker than everywhere else, and super-silky. Mum reckoned that Ellie might get darker as she got older, to match her ears, but Megan wasn't sure. She would be growing for ages, anyway; she was just four months old at the moment. But even though Ellie was only a puppy, she was always bursting with energy.

Ellie stared soulfully at Megan, watching her tape up the box. It looked fun. Her ears twitched, and her tail wagged a little. Perhaps she could jump at that tape? She was never quite sure what was naughty, and sometimes jumping at things got her told off...

Suddenly, Ellie's ears pricked up. She could hear someone coming down the path. Tail wagging, she stood up on the bed to look out of the window, and gave Megan a little warning bark. It was Bella!

Before Bella even had the chance to ring the bell, Megan and Ellie raced out of the room and down the stairs, making for the front door. Ellie won easily. She always did. She was amazingly fast. She scrabbled at the front door with her paws, barking excitedly, until Megan caught up.

"Ssshh! Ellie, ssshh! Come back, look, I can't open the door when you've got your paws on it, can I?"

Ellie scampered back, panting excitedly. She knew Megan's friend Bella, and she hoped this meant a walk after all. She was used to walking with Bella, as Megan and her mum usually picked Bella up on the way to school. Ellie and Megan often walked round the corner to Bella's house when they went to the park too, as Megan's parents didn't like her going on her own, even when she had Ellie with her.

"Hi, Megan! Mum said I could come round and help you pack, if that's OK with your mum and dad?" Bella looked hopefully at Megan's dad, who was struggling into the hall carrying a massive box of china from the kitchen.

"Umph! Fine by me," Dad said, putting down the box carefully. "But make sure you *do* pack, girls, OK? Not just chatting."

Bella stared around Megan's room. "All these boxes!" She slumped down on Megan's bed sadly, and Ellie scrambled up after her to lick her face. "Oof, not so much, Ellie! Oh, Megan, I've known for ages you were going, but it seems so real now."

Megan sat down beside her, and Ellie wriggled happily between them. "I know. Packing makes it seem as though it really is happening. The day after tomorrow..." Megan's voice wobbled, and Ellie turned to lick her too. What was the matter with them both? She looked worriedly from Megan to Bella and back again, making her big puppy ears swing. Something was definitely wrong. Ellie stood up with her paws on Megan's shoulder, and stuffed her cold black nose firmly into Megan's ear. That always made her laugh.

Megan did laugh this time too, and so did Bella, but somehow they still sounded sad.

"I suppose at least we can send each other emails," Bella said, reaching out to stroke Ellie, and Megan nodded.

"And we can phone." Megan laughed. "Mum said she thought they might have to get me my own phone line, or they'd never get to use the phone themselves! It won't be the same as taking Ellie to the park with you, though."

Ellie stood on the bed, listening to them with her head on one side. Something was definitely going on.

"I'm going to miss her too," Bella agreed, tickling Ellie's ears. "You know Mum still won't let me get a dog because she says we haven't got the time to look after one. Now I won't even be able to share Ellie with you. And she's growing so quickly. I probably won't recognize her soon."

Ellie wagged her tail delightedly

as Bella fussed over her.

"I'll email you loads of photos," Megan promised. "And you're coming to stay. Mum and Dad are going to get me a sleepover bed that slides under mine. Ellie can be half your dog again then."

"You'd better record her bark for me, too," Bella reminded her. "I'll never get out of the house for school in the morning without Ellie barking outside the gate."

Ellie yawned. Megan and Bella kept fiddling around with those boxes and talking, and no one was taking her for a walk. She was bored. She slid off the bed and squeezed underneath it. There were always interesting things to play with under there…

"I knew it!" Megan's dad put his head round the door five minutes later. "You two are sitting there chatting, instead of filling boxes."

"Sorry!" Megan and Bella jumped up, and Megan grabbed a pair of trainers and stuffed them quickly into a box, just to look busy.

"And what's Ellie doing under there?" Dad asked, peering round the end of Megan's bed.

Ellie crept out from under the bed looking rather guilty, with half a roll of brown packing tape attached to her whiskers. It was very chewy, though she didn't really like the taste, and it seemed to have stuck...

"Naughty Ellie!" Megan giggled. "Sorry, Dad. I'll clean her up…"

Dad shook his head. "Honestly, after she ate your mum's shoe yesterday, you'd think she'd have had enough of chewing things. Just keep an eye on her, OK?"

Megan nodded apologetically, and started to peel the tape off Ellie's muzzle. "Silly dog," she muttered lovingly, as Ellie squirmed. "Yes, I know it's not nice, but you can't go round with parcel tape all over you. There!"

After that the girls made a real effort to get on with packing, and for the next hour they hardly even chatted at all.

Ellie whined miserably. After Megan had taken the tape away and told her off, she'd sat so patiently, waiting for someone to play with her, or take her for a walk, or at least stroke her. But Megan and Bella just kept taking things off the shelves and putting them into those strange-smelling boxes. Ellie didn't like it. This was her room, and it was changing. She liked it the way it was before.

"Oh, Ellie, are you bored?" Megan picked her up, hugging her gently. "I wish I could play with you too. But we won't be much longer."

"Actually, I told Mum I'd be back around now," said Bella, hugging Megan and Ellie both at the same time. "I can't believe you've only got tomorrow left!" She gulped. "I wish Mum hadn't arranged for us to go and see my cousins, not on your last day. Call me soon? Promise! Bye, Megan!" Then she dashed out of the room and down the stairs, almost slamming the front door behind her.

Megan sat down limply on her bed, looking round at the piles of boxes, all labelled by Bella in her favourite glittery felt tips with her best spelling, which was dreadful. "It's going to be brilliant," she told Ellie again, but this time she didn't feel quite so sure.

Chapter Two

Packing up had been an adventure to start with, but by the second day, everyone was starting to get grumpy. It was such a huge job. The removals van was coming early the next morning, and everything had to be packed up by then. Megan could tell that her mum was panicking that they wouldn't be ready in time.

She was trying to stay out of the way as much as possible, but it wasn't easy with Ellie. Mum and Dad were far too busy to take her for a proper walk, and Megan wasn't allowed to go out on her own, so Ellie was full of energy, and she couldn't work it off properly. Already that morning she'd chewed a roll of bubble wrap into tiny pieces all over the living room floor, and she kept managing to be in everyone's way.

"Mum, stop!" Megan yelled, as her mum lowered a box of books on to the hall floor.

"What? What is it?" Her mum straightened up, red-faced with effort, and peered worriedly over the top of the huge box.

"You were just about to squish Ellie with that!" Megan helped her mum put the box down on top of another one, then pointed to the space she'd been aiming for. Ellie was sitting there, wagging her tail and looking very pleased with herself.

Mum sighed. "You're going to have to take her into the garden. I'm sorry, Megan, but Ellie's going to get hurt in a minute. She's better off outside."

"Come on, Ellie!" Megan tried to sound enthusiastic as she led Ellie out into the garden. She'd found the red-and-white-striped knotted rope toy that Bella had given Ellie for Christmas in her basket, so at least they could play.

Ellie loved racing up and down the garden after the rope, it was her favourite toy, although she didn't see why she always had to give it back to Megan after she'd fetched it. It was much more fun to chew it to bits. She shook her head vigorously as Megan tugged at the toy, laughing.

"Give it here, you silly girl! I'm going to throw it again!"

"Megan, can you come here a moment!" It was Mum, calling from inside. With everyone already a bit grumpy, she knew she'd better go and see what Mum wanted, rather than pretend she hadn't heard.

"I'll be back in a minute," she promised Ellie, and dashed inside.

Ellie shook the toy a few more times and growled at it, in case it was thinking of fighting back. At last she dropped it on the grass, nosing it hopefully. Where was Megan? This game wasn't as much fun without her. Ellie left the toy and trotted up the garden to the back door.

The door was closed, but Ellie scrambled up the back step, anyway. The door didn't always shut properly, and sometimes she could open it, if she nudged it hard with her nose at just the right place. Ellie pushed at the door. She wagged her tail proudly as it swung open and trotted inside.

Ellie wandered along the hallway, listening for Megan. Ah! That was her voice, coming from upstairs. She bounded up the stairs to find her.

Unfortunately, Megan's dad was coming down the stairs, with his arms full of pictures from the bedrooms that he needed to bubble-wrap.

Ellie yowled as he accidentally trod on her paw, and tried to shoot off through his legs.

Megan's dad stumbled down the stairs, twisting his ankle. He landed painfully at the bottom.

Clutching his ankle, he looked up to see Ellie staring down at him.

"That stupid dog!" he yelled. "Megan! Ellie just tripped me up on the stairs. You're supposed to be watching her! I thought Mum told you to put her outside."

Megan and her mum had heard the crash, and they were already running along the landing.

"She didn't mean to!" Megan protested, hurrying to pick up Ellie, who was whimpering in fright. "I'm sorry, Dad, she *was* outside. I can't have shut the back door properly – it wasn't her fault. Are you OK?"

"No," her father muttered crossly, stretching his ankle. "Take that dog outside, now. Ow!"

Megan carried Ellie back into the garden. The little dog was shivering. She wasn't used to being shouted at, and she'd never heard Megan's dad sound so cross. Megan sat down on the garden bench and cuddled Ellie, whispering soothing words. "Ssshh, he didn't mean it. I'm sorry, Ellie, I should have made sure you couldn't get back in."

Ellie snuggled into her fleecy top, still shaking. At least Megan wasn't angry with her. She whined with pleasure as Megan stroked her ears.

She knew Megan would always be there to look after her.

Chapter Three

Ellie rested her chin on Megan's shoulder, as she lovingly stroked her head over and over.

"Megan!" Mum was calling from inside. Megan stood up slowly, carrying Ellie. She was growing so fast! She had been so small when they got her, it had been easy to hold her like this. But now she was getting to be a real weight.

"Oof, Ellie, my arms are going to fall off," Megan teased her lovingly, as she carried her up the garden. She felt Ellie tense up a little as they went into the kitchen to join Mum and Dad. Obviously she remembered Dad shouting at her. "Hey, ssshhh, it's OK," she whispered. But Ellie buried her nose in Megan's neck and whimpered.

"Is Ellie all right?" Mum asked. "She didn't get hurt too, did she?"

Megan shook her head. "No, I think she's just a bit upset. She didn't know what was going on. I'm really sorry she tripped you up, Dad. How's your ankle?"

Dad had it propped up on the chair in front of him, covered by a bag of frozen peas. "I'll live. But this has made us think, Megan. Mum and I have talked it over, and we're sure it's the right thing to do now…"

"What is?" Megan asked cautiously. From the way Mum and Dad were looking, she had a feeling it was going to be something she wouldn't like.

"Ellie's really been getting in the way while we've been packing, Megan," Mum explained. "It's going to be the same when the removal men are loading up, and when we're unpacking at the new house, too. It's just not practical having a puppy around. Dad could have been hurt really badly."

"She didn't mean to," Megan pleaded. "She's only little. She wasn't trying to be naughty."

"We know that, but we're so busy, and no one has the time to exercise Ellie properly right now. So she's even bouncier and sillier than usual! Aren't you, hey?" Dad reached out very gently to stroke the puppy. "Oh dear, I really did frighten her," he said sadly, as he saw Ellie's eyes widen nervously as he came close. "It isn't fair on her."

Megan gulped. She could see that they were right – she could hardly argue that Ellie wasn't getting in the way, when Dad was sitting there with a hurt ankle. "But, what are you going to do?" she whispered. "You're not going to make us give her back to Mrs Johnston, are you?" Mrs Johnston was the breeder who had sold Ellie to them. She felt tears starting to well up in her eyes. "Please don't say we have to give her back!" she choked out. "It wasn't her fault, I'll be more careful, I promise!"

"Megan, Megan, calm down! Of course we're not sending Ellie back."

Mum laughed, hugging her and Ellie. "This is only for a few days while we move. We don't want to get rid of Ellie, but when we first started planning the move, your gran said she could help out and have Ellie for a bit if we needed her to. So I rang Gran just now, and she said she'd love to have her. She'll drive up and get Ellie, and take her back to Woodlands Cottage until we've settled in a bit, just for a couple of days. We'll pick her up on Tuesday."

"We're all going to be so busy, you'll hardly notice she's gone," Dad said encouragingly.

Megan held Ellie tightly, feeling the warm weight in her arms. She didn't want to send Ellie away. Not when she was already upset. She was sure Ellie would hate it.

"She won't understand," she said sadly. "I know she loves Gran, but she's never stayed with her. She's never stayed anywhere without me! She'll think I've abandoned her... She's really confused with all the packing already, and she doesn't understand what's going on. Couldn't I just be really, really careful and keep her in the garden and not let her get in the way?" Megan begged. "I know Gran will look after her, but Ellie's used to having me. She'll be miserable somewhere else. And Gran's got a cat – that's not going to work! Sid will hate having Ellie in the house!"

Megan looked down at the puppy. Ellie quite liked chasing cats...

"I'm sure your gran will sort them out," Dad said, smiling. "Sid and Ellie will probably be curled up on the sofa together by the time we go and pick Ellie up."

Megan shook her head disbelievingly. "Please…?" she whispered.

Mum sighed. "I'm sorry, Megan. We've already had one accident. And I nearly squashed Ellie with that box this morning. This just isn't the right place for a puppy right now. And the new house, too. We don't really know what it's like – there might be all sorts of places where she could get herself into trouble. We need to check everything out first to make sure she's safe."

Ellie gave an anxious little whine. She could feel that Megan wasn't happy, and she didn't like it. She licked Megan's cheek lovingly and looked at her with big, worried eyes.

Megan pressed her cheek gently against Ellie's soft ears. It wasn't just Ellie who was going to hate this. Megan had been counting on having Ellie to cheer her up over the next couple of days. It was going to be so hard to leave her old home and her best friend. And now it looked like she was going to have to do it all on her own.

Gran drove up from Westbury later that afternoon to pick Ellie up. Ellie had a special dog cage for travelling, and it just about fitted on the back seat of Gran's car. Megan carefully packed up Ellie's basket and blanket, and her bowls and food – including her favourite bone-shaped biscuits. Then there was a bagful of toys, her lead, her blanket – the list went on and on.

"Goodness," Gran murmured. "How many dogs am I looking after?"

"Thanks so much for doing this," said Megan's mum. "It's a huge help."

Ellie was trotting backwards and forwards after Megan as she carried all her things to make a pile in the hall. She was very confused about what was going on, but she'd seen Megan's dad moving her travel cage into Gran's car, so she thought she and Megan must be going somewhere with Gran. They had driven out for special walks in the woods with her before. It must be that. Though Ellie didn't see why she would need her basket and everything else just to go out for the day.

"Right." Gran finished her cup of tea. "We'd better be off then, if we don't want to get back too late. We'll see you all on Tuesday." She hugged Megan. "Oh, I'm so excited about having you all living so close. It's going to be lovely."

Megan hugged her back. She was excited too, but she couldn't help worrying about Ellie. "Gran, you will make sure she's not lonely tonight, won't you? She usually sleeps on my bed," she reminded her anxiously.

"I'll do my best," Gran promised. "I think Sid would leave home if a dog came and tried to sleep on my bed with him, but how about I give Ellie a hot water bottle?"

Megan nodded sadly, as she pictured Ellie spending the night on her own.

"It's only for two days, Megan,"

Dad said, putting an arm around her shoulders. "Ellie will be fine."

Ellie hopped into her cage happily enough, expecting Megan to come and sit next to her on the back seat. She would probably waggle her fingers through the door and tickle her ears.

But Gran was getting into the car without Megan. Ellie looked around anxiously, and barked to tell her she'd made a mistake. Gran looked back over her shoulder, and smiled. "It's all right, Ellie. Shh-shh. Don't worry, we'll see Megan again soon."

Ellie stared back at her. Yes, *Megan*. Gran must know what was wrong. Why were they going without Megan? She felt the vibrations as Gran started the car and howled in despair. Megan was being left behind! Ellie stood up on her hind legs in the cage, trying to look out of the window, but she could only see the side of the car and Gran's seat in front.

Megan was clinging to her mum's arm, trying to stop herself racing after Ellie and yelling at Gran to stop the car. "Oh, Mum, listen to her howling," she said miserably. "She's so upset. Does she really have to go to Gran's?"

Her mum just hugged her.

Ellie couldn't see Megan, but she could hear her, and she sounded unhappy. She scrabbled frantically at the bars of her cage with her paws, desperate to get back to Megan.

As the car pulled away down the road, Ellie barked and barked.

At last, when it hurt to bark any

more, she stopped. She pressed her nose against the door of the travel cage.

Gran had taken her away from Megan, and Megan hadn't wanted her to go. Of course she hadn't! Ellie was Megan's dog. Ellie didn't understand what was going on, but she was absolutely certain about one thing.

She had to get back to Megan.

At Gran's house, everything smelled different. Ellie had been there before, but only with Megan, when it had been fun. Gran was doing her best – she'd taken Ellie for a walk when they first arrived, to stretch her legs after being shut up in the car. But Ellie had trailed along behind her with her ears drooping, and in the end Gran had turned back.

But it was worse in the house. Ellie didn't want to be here, and she *hated* cats. Sid was huge and black and old, and very grumpy. He didn't like dogs at all, and he really didn't like dogs who barked and jumped around all over the place. He stood on the back of an armchair and hissed angrily when he first saw Ellie. With all his fur standing up like that and his tail fluffed up like a brush, Sid was nearly as big as she was.

Gran carefully made sure they were kept apart after that, shutting Ellie in the kitchen. But then the phone rang, and she forgot to close the kitchen door when she came out to the hall to answer it. Ellie trotted out after her – she might not want to be here, but Gran was her one link with Megan.

Sid was sitting in the middle of the hallway like a furry black rock.

Ellie bounced at him bravely and barked, but Sid shot forwards and scraped his claws across her nose. Ellie yelped. She'd chased cats before, or tried to anyway – Megan didn't like her chasing things. But the cats had never fought back before. She stared at Sid worriedly, and he hissed again. It was a clear warning.

Ellie crept behind the sofa and stayed there, sulking, until Gran tempted her out with a handful of bone-shaped biscuits, the ones that Megan always gave her. Even those just made her miss Megan more. Gran took her back into the kitchen away from Sid and tried to make a big fuss of her, but Ellie didn't really want to play. She was too confused.

Perhaps Megan would come and get her soon? She had been here with Megan before, after all. And she definitely remembered Sid, and the way this house smelled so strongly of cat. Megan must be coming later, Ellie decided hopefully. Every time footsteps went past on the pavement outside she pricked up her ears and wagged her tail. But as the afternoon wore on, she stopped bothering. It never was Megan, and now it was getting dark.

She padded over to her basket and stared at it miserably. If Megan was coming to get her, she wouldn't need her basket. Her food bowls were here too, and her toys. Why would they be here if Megan was coming to take her home?

"Can I talk to Ellie, Gran?" Megan asked, gripping the phone tightly.

"I'm not sure that's a very good idea, Megan," Gran said gently. "It might upset her. She'll be fine. I'm going to put a hot water bottle in her basket, and she's got her blanket and all her usual things. I expect she'll have settled down by the morning."

Which means she hasn't settled down now, Megan thought unhappily as she said goodbye. Ellie was hating being at Gran's, just as Megan had thought she would.

They were having fish and chips for tea, as a treat, so they didn't have to cook, but Megan hardly ate anything.

It wasn't the same without Ellie lurking hopefully under the table in case anyone dropped a chip.

She was feeling so miserable she went to bed early, but it took her ages to get to sleep – her room was full of boxes, and they all looked strange and gloomy in the dark. *Only till Tuesday*, Megan told herself. *Today's Sunday. Tuesday afternoon, I'll have Ellie back.*

That night, Ellie was left alone in Gran's kitchen. She had her own familiar basket and her blanket, which was wrapped round a cosy hot water bottle, but she was still desperately homesick.

She whined unhappily for a long while, but Gran didn't come down. Ellie was tired, but her basket felt wrong with the hot water bottle in it. It had cooled down now, and it sloshed and wobbled when she moved. Ellie tried to scrabble it out, but it was heavy, so she picked it up in her teeth and dragged it instead. Still it wouldn't budge. She tugged again and the water started to leak out over her blanket.

Ellie howled. Why had Megan abandoned her?

Chapter Four

Ellie woke up in her damp basket. She eyed the hot water bottle worriedly. People didn't like it when she chewed things. She looked up anxiously as the kitchen door opened, wondering if Gran would be very cross.

But she only laughed. "Oh dear, they did say you liked chewing things at the moment. It's all right, Ellie, I know you didn't mean to be naughty. It was probably silly of me to let you have it. I just didn't think. Don't be sad, little one, you'll see Megan again soon."

Ellie stared up at Gran with mournful eyes, as she tidied up her damp things. Even though Gran was being friendly, she didn't want to stay here. If only she could go back home to Megan.

Ellie was good at finding things, and she was best at finding Megan. She smelled special, and Ellie could always find her. She knew when Megan was coming home from school – she could just feel it. She somehow knew when it was time to go and sit by the door, so she could be there to see Megan as soon as she got inside.

So it would be no problem to find Megan, Ellie was sure. But finding her meant she had to get out first, and she wasn't at all sure about that.

Gran fed Ellie, then let Sid into the kitchen to give him breakfast. After that, she left the door open so Ellie could get out of the kitchen too. Gran watched them anxiously, but this time the cat and the puppy stayed out of each other's way.

After a while, Ellie crept out of the kitchen, watching carefully for Sid. She was fairly sure he was in his favourite place – on the back of the sofa, so he could look out of the window and see exactly what was going on in the street.

The front door was very big and very solid. It had a handle, which Ellie couldn't reach, even standing on her hind legs. The letter box was at the bottom of the door, but even though she could get her claws into it to scratch it open, it was only big enough for her nose and even that hurt. Ellie sat staring at the door hopelessly, then she gave her ears a determined shake. If she couldn't open it, she would just have to wait until someone opened it for her.

She hung around the hallway all morning, waiting for the door to be opened and half-playing with her squeaky fish toy.

She was just scrambling underneath a chest of drawers, trying to reach the squeaky fish, when there was the shrill sound of the doorbell. Ellie jumped, banging her head on the bottom of the chest.

She could hear someone shifting around on the doorstep. This was her chance!

Ellie wriggled herself round under the chest, so that her nose was sticking out, and watched as Gran hurried to answer the door. It was the postman with a parcel. Gran opened the door wider to take the sheet of paper she needed to sign, and Ellie's ears pricked up as she saw what was beyond it. Gran's didn't have a fenced-in front garden like Megan's house did, just a flower bed and then straight on to the pavement. As Gran turned away from the door to rest the sheet of paper on the very chest Ellie was hiding under, Ellie darted out of the door.

Ellie's heart was thumping as she hid herself behind an enormous clump of stripy leaves under the front window. She had expected the postman to see her and shout, and maybe try to catch her, but he was too busy chatting away with Gran. Still, Ellie was sure Gran would see her if she tried to run down the street now. Hiding was best. She watched anxiously as Gran gave the sheet back, and the door began to close. Was she going to notice?

Some strange sense made her look up just then, and she nearly gave herself away with a yelp.

Sid was staring down at her from his perch on the back of the sofa. He knew she was there. What if he mewed and Gran discovered she'd got out?

Ellie watched Sid nervously. Should she run now, and see if she could get far enough away in the few seconds she had left? But Sid wasn't meowing to get Gran's attention. He was sitting very still, just watching with disapproving eyes, the tip of his tail twitching very slightly.

The front door slammed shut. Ellie gulped. *He wasn't going to stop her.*

She supposed it made sense. He didn't want her in his house any more than she wanted to be there. Ellie wagged her tail at him gratefully, and sneaked out from behind the bush and on to the pavement.

She needed to get away from Gran's house fast, before Gran realized what had happened and came to find her. Ellie looked around, her tail wagging very slightly. She couldn't help but be excited. She was heading back to Megan! She was going to find her, all by herself!

She was going home.

Ellie skittered quickly across the road, making for a little lane with high hedges that led down between some of the houses. She'd be out of sight from Gran's house quickly here, she was sure.

Once she was in
the lane she raced as
fast as she could.
They had gone
down here on the
walk yesterday; it
was brambly and
overgrown, with lots
of hiding places.

Finally she ran out of breath and
collapsed, panting, underneath a
tangle of brambles. She lay in the leafy
dimness, breathing fast, and loving the
feeling of being out on her own. Walks
with Megan were the best thing, of
course, but it was fun not to have a lead
on and to be able to go where she
liked. The bramble bush smelled nice.
Earthy, but sweet at the same time.

Ellie tried to work out which way she should go next. Where was Megan? Which way?

She rested her nose on her paws. It wasn't that she was going to sniff Megan out exactly, that would be silly, she was much too far away for that. This was different from finding Megan's scent. It was more of a feel. Megan – and home – was that way.

Ellie wriggled eagerly out from under the brambles and set off down the lane. She knew it was going to be a long way – longer than any walk she'd done before – but she wasn't scared. She was Megan's dog, not Gran's, and she was meant to be with Megan.

Back at the house, Gran was searching anxiously for Ellie. She hadn't missed her until a few minutes ago, when she had put out Ellie's lunch, and she was hoping that the puppy was hiding in the house somewhere.

"Ellie! Ellie! Here, girl! Where are you?"

Gran crouched down to check behind the sofa, in case Sid had frightened her again. The cat was still curled up on the back of the sofa.

"Where can she be, Sid?" Gran muttered worriedly. "Oh, she can't have got out when the postman came? I would have seen her, surely. And that's the only time I've opened the door. But then where is she? I've looked everywhere."

Gran thought sadly of Megan – they'd be leaving their old house about now, she expected. Megan would be so excited; how could she spoil their moving day by telling them Ellie was lost? But if she didn't find the little dog soon, she would have to.

Sid followed as she went out into the hallway and opened the front door. Gran looked anxiously up and down the street, while Sid coiled round her ankles, purring lovingly.

He really didn't like dogs in his house.

The lane led out on to a main road. It was a busy road, and it didn't have wide pavements for people and dogs to walk on, like the ones Ellie was used to. She stood hesitating on the little patch of ground where the lane and the road met, and watched the cars whooshing past. She wasn't supposed to go near cars. She had been very carefully trained to sit and wait at the edge of the pavement until Megan said to walk.

Cautiously, Ellie stretched out one paw on to the road, then jumped back with a frightened yelp as a car shot by in a speeding rush of air. Ellie looked around and decided that she wouldn't cross, even though the lane went on over the other side of the road. She would walk along the edge of the road instead. She was fairly sure she would still be going the right way. She set off, but the edge of the road was only a narrow fringe of dusty grass below the hedges. Every time a car went past it ruffled Ellie's fur, and the tyres screeched and scared her. She kept jumping into the hedge in fright.

Ellie was cowering in the hedge waiting for an enormous lorry to thunder past, when she realized that just in front of her was a hole. It was a gap in the thick hedge, leading away from this horrible, frightening road! Ellie darted through it and found herself in a field. This was much better.

There were no cars, only long grass that was fun to run through. Ellie darted across the field happily. This was much the best way to go – no more roads, she decided, at least until she got close to Megan's house, where there were roads all around.

Ellie reached the hedge to the next field and nosed along it, looking for a good place to scramble through. It was thick and prickly, but suddenly she found a small tunnel. Ellie wriggled into it – then stopped.

She was stuck! Her collar had caught on something. She pulled frantically, but the collar only tightened around her neck until it hurt. She tried again, and again, but she couldn't break the collar, or the branch it had caught on.

At last, worn out from pulling, she sat still, whimpering a little. Something else must use this tunnel, and she didn't want to be here when it came back. Pulling at the collar just wasn't going to work – but when Megan had first put it on her, she had managed to get it off, hadn't she? It had been a little big and it wasn't now, but surely if she really tried? Instead of pulling forwards, Ellie wriggled backwards, twisting her neck so that she reversed out of her collar, wrenching it over her ears.

Ellie fell backwards, rolling over in the leaves. She had done it! Her ears felt like she had half pulled them off, but although her collar was still stuck in the hedge, she wasn't. Ellie stepped out into the next field, her legs shaky with relief.

The next hedge was easy; she edged through it on her tummy and hardly even caught her fur. But as she wriggled through she could smell something strange on the other side... The field she came out in was full of cows. Ellie had only ever seen cows at a distance, and she'd never walked through a field full of them. They were very large. She stood watching for a moment, but the cows didn't seem to notice her. Most of them were grazing, though a few were lying down quietly.

She took a cautious step out into the field, then started to trot quickly across it, keeping herself low to the ground and hoping the cows wouldn't notice her. The problem was that they were scattered everywhere, so she had to go close to a few of them. Luckily, she scampered past so quickly that they hardly had time to turn their huge heads before she'd left them behind. But a few of them got nervously to their feet at the sight of the dog.

Ellie was nearly at the far hedge when she heard a heavy, lumbering tread behind her. She darted a look over her shoulder, her heart suddenly racing at double speed. An enormous black-and-white cow was thundering towards her, head lowered to show off short but business-like horns. It was staring angrily straight at Ellie, and it snorted at her in fury.

Ellie ran faster than she ever had before, racing at top speed for the hedge. She could feel the cow's hot breath as it huffed and blew behind her. Its enormous hooves trampled the grass, inches away from her tail. Ellie let out a frightened bark. She had to go faster!

Chapter Five

Megan stood in her bedroom, surrounded by boxes. It felt so strange that she had been doing just the same thing a couple of hours ago, but in her old house. There her room had looked really sad, like the end of something, but here it was a new start. It was so exciting! She just wished she had Ellie here to see everything too. She peered out of her window at the big garden, sloping down to a stream, and the woods on the other side. Tomorrow she could go and explore it all with Ellie!

Megan was suddenly desperate to talk to Gran and find out if Ellie was OK. She hurried downstairs.

"Dad, can I borrow your mobile?" Megan asked, bursting into the kitchen.

But Dad was already on the phone, looking anxious.

Megan made a "sorry!" face, but Dad only smiled at her distractedly.

"What's the matter?" Megan asked. Even the air in the kitchen felt full of worry.

"It's Gran on the phone," Mum said quietly, putting her arm around Megan. "She called to say that she thinks Ellie slipped out of the door this morning. But she's sure Ellie can't have got far."

"But, but – where can she have gone?" Megan asked, in a frightened whisper. "She hardly knows anywhere round there. She'll get lost!"

Megan sat down at the table, feeling sick. She would never have let Ellie go if she'd thought this might happen. How could Gran have let her get out?

Dad ended the call, then sat down next to her and covered her hand with his. "Gran's going to come round and pick you up so you can go and look for Ellie with her."

Megan nodded, feeling a little bit better. But it was so hard to think of Ellie, lost and lonely and scared. She had to try very hard not to cry.

Gran hugged her when she arrived, and she looked so upset that Megan forgot to be cross and just hugged her back.

"We'll find her, Megan," she promised. "I'm so sorry. She must have slipped out when the postman came.

I just didn't see. She's probably gone off exploring in the woods. The moment she hears your voice, she's sure to come running."

They drove back to Gran's, and then set off into the woods that ran behind the cottages, calling and calling.

But Ellie didn't come running, as Megan had so hoped she would. The daffodils were flowering and it was so beautiful – Megan had been looking forward to walking here with her dog so much. But all she could think about now was how scared Ellie would be out here on her own. She was still so little, and most of their walks were in the park. Ellie could get trapped in a rabbit hole, or fall in a stream! Megan sniffed hard, and rubbed her sleeve across her eyes.

"Let's go and try down the lane," Gran suggested, looking around one last time. "I just don't think she can be here, she would have heard us calling."

They found no sign of Ellie in the lane either. They went all the way down to the road, and Megan watched the cars speeding by. What if Ellie had been run over? She had tried so hard to teach her to be careful, but she was only a puppy, and she might easily have run into the road.

"I don't think she'd come along here," Gran said, hugging her. "Don't worry, Megan. Look, Ellie would be frightened of those cars if she was on her own. She wouldn't try to cross. Come on, we'll go back home. I've already asked my neighbours, but we'll go and ask round the village if anyone's seen her. Someone's sure to have done."

But Gran looked worried. It was as though Ellie had simply disappeared.

Ellie made a big leap and shot into the hedge, the cow snorting angrily behind her. It lowered its horns, as Ellie fought and scrambled her way through the twigs. She gave a yelp of relief as she struggled out into tufts of long grass on the other side of the hedge.

The cow snorted grumpily and lumbered away, and Ellie collapsed panting on the soft grass. She'd left her collar in the last hedge, but it felt like she'd left half her fur in this one.

Now that she was safely away from the cows, Ellie realized how hungry she was, and thirsty too. She hadn't had lunch, and it felt a long way past lunchtime now. But although the sun was sinking, it was still warm. The air felt sticky, and black clouds were gathering behind the trees.

The quiet lane was leading to houses, just a few, but there might be some food around, Ellie thought hopefully. And somewhere to rest. She didn't want to stay out in the open all night. She didn't like that strange close feeling in the air. It made her fur feel prickly.

"Mum rang the police just now and reported her missing." Megan gulped. "She's been gone all day, Bella! The policeman said it's good that she's microchipped, because if someone brings her in, they can check. Mum gave them the new address. Gran and I searched and searched, and then we made posters on her computer. We've stuck them up everywhere, but no one's called. I wish you were here to help us look." Megan was sitting in her new bedroom, borrowing Dad's mobile to call Bella. She hated having to tell her that Ellie was missing. It made it seem even more real.

"Oh, Megan!" Bella sounded almost as upset as she was. "Have you been all through those woods you told me about?"

"We've searched the woods twice, and Mum says I can't go again now, it's getting dark," Megan said sadly. "I just want her back. She'll be so scared, Bella. I hate thinking of her all on her own."

The first house Ellie came to kept its bins tightly closed. She headed on past. There was a good smell coming from somewhere close. Bread, she thought, sneaking carefully down the side of a house and squirming under an iron gate. Yes! Bread crusts, scattered all over a patio around a bird table. Ellie gobbled them greedily. She was so glad to find some food that she didn't notice she was being watched. The slam of a door made her jump back in fright. An elderly lady came out, looking cross and waving a broom. She poked it at Ellie, who skittered back in horror.

"Shoo! Out of here, bad dog! Don't you scare away my birds! Shoo! Go home!" And she banged the brush on the paving stones, making Ellie squeak with fright. The puppy shot across the garden towards the gap under the gate, wriggling out and away as quickly as she could.

Once she was safely a few houses away, she hid under a car, shivering. She hadn't known the bread was special; she was only hungry. Ellie whimpered. She wanted Megan back. Then she shook her ears determinedly. She was on her way to Megan. She had a feeling that she had walked along this lane before, with Megan and Gran when they were out together. It was definitely on the way home. She poked out her nose from under the car, checking for the old lady, but there was no one around.

It was getting dark, though. She wanted to keep going, but the stormy feeling in the air was getting stronger, and she could hear low growls of thunder. It made the fur stand up on her back. She would have to find somewhere to stop for the night. All of a sudden, the greyish sky split with a bright flash of lightning, and a heartbeat later thunder crashed down. Ellie howled, and dived through a garden gate.

She raced into the garden, looking round desperately for somewhere to hide from those horrible noises. A house! A little wooden house, just here in the corner, just the right size for a dog. There were spotted curtains blowing in the window, and the door was open the tiniest crack. Ellie nosed at it, pushing it wider, and sneaked inside. There was even a cushion on the floor, along with a scatter of crayons. Ellie collapsed on to it gratefully and closed her eyes. It seemed a very long time since she'd run away that morning.

Soon Ellie was fast asleep.

A few miles away, Megan was lying awake. She wasn't really scared of thunder, not when she was safe inside. But tonight it was terrifying. She kept imagining Ellie outside, frightened by the growling thunder. What if she was hurt? What if she was hiding under a tree to get out of the rain, and the tree was struck by lightning?

Megan watched the rain beating against the windows, and shivered. It was a long time before she finally huddled under her bedclothes and drifted off into a troubled sleep.

The creak of the wooden door opening woke Ellie with a start. She shot upright, backing nervously into the corner of the playhouse.

A little boy was staring at her. He looked just as amazed as she did.

"A dog!" he breathed delightedly. "A dog's come!"

He sounded friendly, and Ellie relaxed a little, but she didn't go closer. Most children she met with Megan loved her and wanted to stroke her, but Megan wouldn't let her jump up at children, or even sniff them. One little girl had seen her walking past, and then Ellie had gone to sniff her hand, and she'd squealed. Ellie had felt quite hurt. So now she watched this little boy carefully.

"Hello, dog…" He was crouching down now, staring into her eyes, and Ellie was sure that this one wasn't going to cry. "I'm William. Have you come to stay? Are you going to live in my house?" He sounded very excited. "I know! You're hungry! Grandad's dog is always hungry." He leaned closer, and whispered, "Mummy's on the phone. I was having breakfast, but I came out when she wasn't looking. You can have my breakfast." He scrambled out of the little house and dashed away.

Ellie stood there blinking, not quite sure what was going on. She pattered over to the door, and peered out. William was coming back, more slowly now, his dark head bent earnestly over a bowl, with something balanced on the edge of it.

"There! My Weetabix. I've already had two, so you can have that one. And this is a bacon sandwich. I don't like bacon anyway."

Ellie could smell the bacon. After nothing but stale bread crusts since yesterday, it smelt like heaven. She trotted over to him and took it delicately from his hand as he held it out to her. It disappeared in about three bites.

"Wow, you are hungry." William sounded impressed.

Ellie sighed with pleasure, licking the bacon from round her whiskers, and looked hopefully at the bowl.

"Oh! Do you like Weetabix too?" He put the bowl down on the ground for her and watched hopefully.

Ellie sniffed at it with interest. Oh, yes, she recognized this. She had proper dog food at home now, but when she'd been very small she'd had this too, for breakfast. She liked it. She gulped it down, licking the bowl out thoroughly, then sat down, scratching her ear with one hind paw. She always did that after meals. It felt good.

William laughed. "Funny dog," he said, crouching down to stroke her gently.

Ellie closed her eyes, and leaned against him happily. He reminded her of Megan, even though he was so little. She would see Megan soon, she thought excitedly.

"Oh!" William straightened up. "Mum's calling me. I have to go.

I'm going to ask her if you can stay! Mum! Mum!" He dashed back to the house, and Ellie watched the kitchen door swing shut behind him. She would have liked to stay with him for longer, but she was sure she wasn't that far from home now.

She crept past the playhouse and back under the garden gate. She paused for a moment outside William's house, to give him one last grateful bark, then she went on her way.

Chapter Six

A few hours later, Ellie stood looking down into the river. She was sure she had just seen a fish. She had been here once before, one wonderful afternoon when they'd had a picnic, and Mum had told Megan off for feeding her bits of sausage roll. Remembering it made her feel hungry. She had walked a very long way since the bacon sandwich.

Ellie set off again along the riverbank, wondering if she could catch a fish. That one had looked very slippery. And although she loved getting wet, she hadn't had a lot of practice at swimming.

Ah. Maybe this would be better than a fish. Just ahead of her, standing on the riverbank, was a man with a fishing rod, staring out over the water at his float. But what really interested Ellie was his bag of sandwiches, lying by his tackle box.

Ellie sneaked closer, and then darted out from behind a tree and seized a sandwich.

"Hey!" The fisherman shouted crossly, but he couldn't chase her without getting tangled in his line. He was trying to lay it down carefully, but Ellie didn't wait for him. Gripping the sandwich in her teeth, she ran for it, racing away down the overgrown path.

When his shouts died away into the distance, Ellie sat down to eat her prize: a tuna sandwich. So she was having fish after all!

She licked up the last crumbs from the grass and sighed happily. She felt much better now. She stood up and gave herself a brisk shake. It was time to set off home again.

"Hello? Yes, this is Lindsey. Oh!" Mum beckoned frantically to Megan, who was listlessly picking at her tea. She just didn't feel like eating – it made her worry about how hungry Ellie must be, after a day and a half with no food.

"Who is it?" she asked, staring at Mum's excited face. Then she sat up straight, gasping. "Is it the posters? Has someone seen her?"

Mum was nodding. "Yes, yes, a Labrador puppy. Yes, quite small. Let me write that down. By the bridge. Oh dear, I am sorry. And that was this morning? Oh, thank you so much for calling us. Yes, I hope we will too." She ended the call, and turned to

Megan, who was now standing right next to her, trying desperately to hear what the person on the other end of the line had been saying. "That was a man from the village who was fishing down by Selby Bridge this morning. Ellie stole his sandwiches!" Mum hugged her, laughing.

Megan smiled. "I was just thinking about how hungry she must be!"

"Come on, call your dad. Let's go and look for her. It's getting dark, but we should be able to see for a while."

Ellie's paws were aching, but she felt so proud of herself. She had done it. She could see Megan's school playground, and the park was just round the next corner. She was so close! Despite her weariness, she trotted along faster. In a few minutes she would be back with Megan. She was just in time – already it was starting to get dark.

This was her road, and there was her house! Ellie looked carefully up and down the road for cars, then crossed over to her own front gate. She couldn't open it, but it was a pretty iron one that she could slip through, even though it was a tight fit. She stood outside the front door and barked happily. They were going to be so pleased to see her!

No one came to the door, so she scratched at it with her front paws and barked again, louder and louder.

At last she heard
footsteps. Ellie
barked and jumped
delightedly. She was
going to see Megan!
But when the door
opened, it wasn't
Megan. Or even her
mum or dad. There
was a strange woman
standing there,
looking down
at her in
surprise.

Ellie whimpered, tucking her tail between her legs in confusion.

Megan had gone. She had left, and abandoned Ellie with Gran. Megan didn't want her any more.

"What's going on?" A man was coming down the hall now, looking surprised. "Oh! A dog? Has it got a collar?"

"No, I don't think so." The woman bent down to look.

Ellie backed away from the doorstep, miserably. She didn't know what to do. But the woman who'd answered the door followed her, talking gently. "Don't be scared, puppy, are you lost? Oh, look, she's shivering, poor little thing. She's so pretty, and she can't be very old."

The man came out too. "She must have slipped out of someone's house, don't you think? Maybe we'd better keep her for the night. We'll have to put her in the shed, though. Jasper would go crazy if we brought another dog in, and he's already upset about the new house. We can take her round to the police station in the morning, and see if she's been microchipped." And he reached down and scooped Ellie up.

The man carried Ellie round the side of her house, only it wasn't her house any more, and she wasn't even allowed in. They put down a rug for her in the shed, with a bowl of water and some dog biscuits. It was comfortable, but she was in the garden and she was shut up, when she should be inside, upstairs sleeping on Megan's bed.

Her family had gone away and left her. She just didn't understand. Even though Megan's dad had been cross with her, Megan had still cuddled her and talked to her and loved her the same way, hadn't she? Why had Megan left her behind? Had she just forgotten her?

Ellie buried her nose under her paws and whimpered. She'd spent so long trying to get home, and now home wasn't there.

Chapter Seven

Megan woke up and lay staring at the ceiling for a second. It looked wrong. Then she remembered she was in her new house. She felt a rush of excitement, until she looked down at the empty space at the end of her bed and remembered that Ellie was missing. She wished she could just go back to sleep and this would only be a dream.

She had been so hopeful yesterday evening when they'd got the phone call. They'd driven straight down to Selby Bridge, which was on the way back to their old house. It was a beautiful place, and they'd taken Ellie there before for walks. She and Mum and Dad had searched all the way along the riverbank, calling, and banging Ellie's food bowl, something suggested by the friendly policeman that Mum had spoken to on the phone yesterday.

At last Dad had taken her hand. "Megan, it's getting dark. I think we have to stop."

"But we can't! She was here!" Megan had protested.

"We can come back in the morning and look again," Mum promised.

So Megan had to get up now. That man had definitely seen Ellie – there couldn't be two lost Labrador puppies, could there? She climbed out of bed wearily. She felt like she'd been dreaming about Ellie all night. In the worst dream, the puppy had been in the middle of a road, and Megan could hear a car coming. She shivered.

Megan started to pull on her dressing gown, then suddenly she stopped and sat down on her bed again, staring wide-eyed at the photo on the shelf. It was a picture of her and Bella and Ellie playing in their old garden. She reached over and picked it up. How could she have been so stupid? Ellie had been at Selby Bridge. Halfway back to their old house!

Ellie wasn't lost at all. She was trying to go home!

"Mum! Dad!" Megan went racing into their room. "Dad, where's your mobile, we have to call the people at our old house. Ellie's gone home!"

Her parents were still half asleep, and her dad blinked at her wearily. "What do you mean?"

Megan sat down on the edge of the bed and started to explain. "She was really upset about being at Gran's, wasn't she. She didn't understand what was going on. She doesn't know we've moved, Dad! She's trying to get back to our old house! She'd got halfway yesterday morning. She's probably home by now!" Megan suddenly frowned. "Oh, no. She's going to find somebody else in our house." Her voice shook.

Mum sat up. "Megan, I don't think Ellie can have got that far. How could she find the way? It's a lovely idea, but…"

"She got as far as Selby Bridge!" Megan pointed out.

"Yes, I suppose so…"

"You do hear of dogs doing that kind of thing," Dad put in thoughtfully. "Maybe we should ring the house, just in case. But it's too early right now."

Mum and Dad made her wait a whole hour before they called. Megan had walked in circles around the kitchen; she couldn't face breakfast. Now she was pressed close to Dad, trying to hear the phone conversation.

"She came to the door? Last night? No, we hadn't thought of calling you before, it's such a long way, you see. Nearly ten miles! That's wonderful. Yes, yes, of course, I see. I'm sure she would be fine in the shed. Yes, we'll come straight away. We'll see you soon."

"They've found her! They really have! Oh, Dad!" Megan was dancing now, jumping and flinging herself at her parents to hug them. Then she raced to get her boots on. They were going to get Ellie back!

Ellie lay on the rug in the chilly shed, wondering where she should go, now that she didn't have a home any more.

She didn't want to go back to Gran's. Sid didn't like her, and she didn't want to live with him. She would have to find somewhere new.

The problem was, Ellie didn't want anywhere new. She only wanted Megan. But she certainly couldn't stay here. Ellie scrambled over the tangle of old garden equipment that was still cluttering up the shed, sniffing out that fresh, cold breeze. There was a loose board in the wall! Ellie pushed it to one side and started to wriggle through. Her fur felt full of dust and splinters. She squeezed out the other side and shook herself briskly.

The new people had left the side gate open, and Ellie raced out down the side of the house. She didn't want them to shut her up again. She was about to run straight out of the front gate, but something stopped her.

Lying on the path, half-hidden by the bins, was one of her toys. Her favourite toy. The red-and-white-striped knotted rope toy that Bella had given her. Ellie picked it up in her teeth and shook it happily. It was so good to chew, and she loved it when Megan pulled the other end and then they'd play tug-of-war together.

Madly shaking the toy from side to side, Ellie knew, with sudden, happy certainty, that Megan had not left her behind. Not on purpose. Megan loved to play with her, and stroke her, and talk to her.

Ellie trotted determinedly out of her

old front garden, squeezing quickly through the front gate, and set off down the street. She wasn't sure where she was going, but she was not going to give up. She reached the end of the road and looked around thoughtfully. She usually walked down here with Megan to pick up Bella on her way to school.

Bella! Bella loved her, and she loved Megan. Bella would know where Megan was! Ellie raced down the road, yelping with excitement, still carrying the rope toy.

As she turned the corner, she didn't  notice a familiar car driving down the road. The car pulled up outside the house and Megan leaped out. Without waiting for her parents, she went running up the garden path of their old house, and rang and rang on the doorbell.

Chapter Eight

Outside Bella's front gate, Ellie dropped the rope toy, and sat down neatly, just like she always used to. Then she barked loudly, three times.

She waited. She was just about to bark again, when Bella's front door opened, and Bella rushed out on to the path.

"Ellie! I thought it was you barking, but Mum said it couldn't possibly be!

What are you doing here? Megan said on the phone last night someone had seen you at Selby Bridge. How did you get all the way back here?" Bella flung open the gate. "Oh, Ellie, we've all been so worried about you! Come on, Ellie, come! Here, girl!"

Bella held open the gate and beckoned Ellie in.

Ellie picked up her toy and followed her. She trusted Bella not to shut her in a shed. Bella would help her get back to Megan, she was sure.

"Mum, Mum, look! Ellie's here! It was her barking, I told you!" Bella and Ellie dashed down the hall to Bella's mum in the kitchen. "I have to call Megan, please, Mum?"

"Has she come all the way from

Woodlands Cottage? She can't have done, it must be at least ten miles." Bella's mum was staring at Ellie in amazement. "She doesn't have a collar, are you sure this is Ellie? You haven't just stolen someone's dog?"

"Mu-um! Of course it's Ellie! Look, she's carrying the toy that I bought her for Christmas. Besides, only Ellie would know to sit at the gate and bark three times. Oh, they're not answering." Bella put down the phone with a crash and stared at Ellie. "Is it really ten miles? How could she walk that far? And how did she know the way?"

"Well, dogs can be very clever," her mum said doubtfully. "But I don't know, to be honest. Because she was so desperate to find Megan, I suppose."

Ellie barked, her eyes wide with hope. *Megan!* They had definitely said Megan.

"She heard you say it." Bella laughed. "Are you trying to find Megan, Ellie?"

Ellie jumped up with her paws on Bella's knees, and barked and barked, wagging her tail frantically.

"It's OK, Megan will be here soon, I promise. She'll come and get you. Or we could take her to Megan's new house, couldn't we, Mum?"

Her mum frowned. "That might not be a good idea. She could get upset. Why don't we try ringing the house again?"

Bella nodded. "I have missed you, Ellie. But not as much as Megan has.

She's been searching for you all over the place." She stroked Ellie's soft head. "She's going to be so happy to have you back."

Megan sat in the car outside her old house, gulping back tears. Her mum was sitting next to her, trying to calm her down, and her dad was leaning over from the front seat.

"I know it's hard, Megan, but I promise we'll find her. Come on, this is good news. We know she was here last night! That's a really good start."

Megan nodded, but she couldn't stop crying. "She came all this way to find us," she whispered tearfully. "And then there was someone else in her house. Another dog as well! She must have thought we just didn't love her any more. What if she's gone off to find somewhere else to live?"

"I'm sure she won't have," Mum said firmly. "Ellie won't give up. She made it this far, didn't she? She'll be around here somewhere, probably just a bit confused. Let's go and try the park."

But Ellie wasn't in the park, or in any of the streets around their old house. They called, Megan's dad whistled, and they stopped to ask everyone they saw. But there was no trace of her.

"She's gone." Megan had stopped crying now. She was almost too upset to cry. "We had our chance and now we've lost her for ever."

"Megan!" Her mum crouched down and hugged her. "I never thought I'd hear you giving up. You have to keep going – Ellie needs you to find her."

Megan nodded, biting her lip. Her mum was right. Ellie wouldn't give up on her, would she? "Can we go and see Bella? Get her to look out for Ellie? She won't know Ellie's back here, and she could ask people from school if she sees them."

"Good idea," her mum said. "Let's go back to the car – we'll drive round."

Megan rang Bella's doorbell, thinking back to the last time she'd done that – on the final day of school, when Bella had been running so late she hadn't come out of the house when Ellie barked.

She'd been pulling on her coat when she opened the door, and she'd had a piece of toast sticking out of her mouth. She'd fed a little bit of it to Ellie.

Megan blinked. Why was there barking coming from inside Bella's house? She didn't have a dog…

Just then, the door flew open. "I knew it! Did you get my message? I've called about six times! Why didn't you call me back?" Bella's words were falling over each other in excitement, but Megan hardly heard her.

She was hugging Ellie – Ellie who'd leaped into her arms as soon as Bella opened the door. The puppy's paws were on Megan's shoulders in a golden furry hug, and she was licking Megan's face all over.

Megan's parents laughed delightedly, and Bella's mum started telling them about Ellie's sudden appearance.

Megan beamed at Bella. "We didn't get any message, we weren't at home, you see. The people from the new house had found Ellie, but she slipped out of the shed. They had to put her in there because they had a dog too, so – urrgh, Ellie, don't lick my mouth!

So they shut Ellie in, but there's a hole in the shed wall, so she got out. She must have decided to come to you, she knows you really love her. Bella, you found her!" And she hugged Bella too, squidging Ellie in between them.

"No, she found me," Bella giggled. "She turned up and barked outside the gate. I thought I was dreaming!"

"Oh, Ellie, I'm never letting you go anywhere again," Megan gasped in between licks. "You're such a clever, brilliant dog – how did you find your way back here?"

Ellie sighed deeply, and laid her chin on Megan's shoulder. All of a sudden, she felt very, very tired.

It had been a long journey, but now, at last, she was back home with Megan.

The Seaside Puppy
From best-selling author
HOLLY WEBB
Illustrated by Sophy Williams

Monty the
Sad Puppy

From best-selling author
HOLLY WEBB
Illustrated by Sophy Williams

The
Homeless
Kitten

From best-selling author
HOLLY WEBB
Illustrated by Sophy Williams

A Kitten Called Tiger

From best-selling author
HOLLY WEBB
Illustrated by Sophy Williams

HOLLY WEBB

Holly Webb started out as a children's book editor and wrote her first series for the publisher she worked for. She has been writing ever since, with over one hundred books to her name. Holly lives in Berkshire, with her husband and three young sons. Holly's pet cats are always nosying around when she is trying to type on her laptop.

For more information
about Holly Webb visit:

www.holly-webb.com